Last Waltz on the Danube:

THE ETHNIC GERMAN GENOCIDE IN HISTORY AND MEMORY

1944-1948

Ali Botein-Furrevig, Ph.D.

Includes Holocaust and Genocide Educator's Guide

PUBLISHING
MARGATE, NEW JERSEY

Published by:
    ComteQ Publishing
    A division of ComteQ Communications, LLC
    101 N. Washington Ave. • Suite 2B
    Margate, New Jersey 08402
    609-487-9000 • Fax 609-487-9099
    Email: publisher@ComteQpublishing.com
    Website: www.ComteQpublishing.com

ISBN 978-1-935232-59-9

Book & over design by Rob Huberman

Cover Photo: "Shoes on the Danube" by Nikodem Nijaki, 1/1/2012. Creative Commons Attribution-Share Alike 3.0 license. The monument of the same name by Hungarian Sculptor ,Gyula Pauer, is situated on the bank of the Danube River in Budapest. The memorial contains 60 pairs of iron shoes and is dedicated to the victims of the Fascist Arrow Cross Party, who shot the people right into the river, sparing themselves the hard work of burials. The victims had to take their shoes off, since shoes were valuable belongings at the time. Its tragic symbolism, however, extends to ethnic Germans and Jews who were forced into the frozen river and then shot during and after WWII.

Printed in the United States of America

For Jordan and Jennifer
Dedicated to the Lavundi and Karl Families
in
Loving Memory of Wilhelm Stefan Lavundi, Ph.D.
(1937-2010)

With deep affection and gratitude to
Mrs. Katharina Karl Marx, for graciously sharing
her immense knowledge and remarkable story.
and
For my cherished students:
It is said in the Talmud: "And thou shalt teach
thy children that they may remember."

Acknowledgements

I am especially indebted to the following individuals:

John R. Schindler and George Wildmann, for their research and expansive histories of the Donauschwaben people, and for meticulously chronicling their expulsion and genocide from 1944-1948.

Frank Schmidt, for his exhaustive scholarship and articles on the Donauschwaben people and for his numerous translations of German texts in this area of study.

Dr. Jakob Schmidt and his translator **Doris Feldtanzer**, for his detailed history and culture of Batschka Palanka.

Dennis Bauer, for his expertise of, and commitment to, recording the history and genealogy of the Palankan people.

The Donauschwaben Societies of New York, Trenton, and Philadelphia, for their dedication to promoting and archiving Donauschwaben history— and for all they do to preserve their heritage and pass it on to future generations.

Rob Huberman, my publisher, for his creative insights and marketing advice.

Alison Ward, my amazing copy editor, for her meticulous reading of the manuscript.

Philomena Bianca Simonelli, for her friendship and open door. She is always there to make sense out of nonsense over endless cups of black coffee.

Michael Zahler, Professor of History at Ocean County College and Kean University at Ocean (and my loyal sidekick) for his support and for sharing his vast knowledge of the Roman Empire.

And, of course, **Allan Peter Furrevig**, my husband, for his unwavering support of me and for always understanding the endless hours required to teach, research, and write. His sense of humor and common sense perspective always keeps me grounded.

Danube Swabian Associations of America

Dear Dr. Botein:

On behalf of the Danube Swabian Associations of Philadelphia and Vicinity, Trenton, and New York, we want to extend our heartfelt gratitude to you for your scholarly efforts to shed light on a complex period of East European history. You have meticulously researched a little known aspect of World War Two and postwar history with humanitarian commitment, and *sine ira et studio.* During the years 1944-48, thousands of Danube Swabians in Yugoslavia were murdered, interned, sent to the Soviet Union, or starved to death because of their German background. In 1947, the surviving internees were transported north to the camps of Gacovo and Krusivl. From there the escape to Hungary and to the West, where they could be classified as *Displaced Persons,* was easier .Today survivors of this ethnic group can be found all over the world—in the United States, Canada, South America, Australia, New Zealand, and Europe. We are indebted to you for compassionately and lovingly telling the story of our destiny to the world and honoring the memories of those who perished.

Sincerely,
Philadelphia: *Rosalie Matico, President; Fred Gauss, Vice-President; Kathe Marx, Secretary*
Trenton: *Joseph Brandecker, President; Dennis J. Bauer, Vice-President; Hans Martini*
New York: *George Ritter, President; Adam Metzger, Vice-President; Magdalene Metzger, Secretary*

Table of Contents

Author's Preface

On a glorious spring afternoon a few years back as I was walking across campus, a Jewish colleague caught up with me. "I'm just curious," she began, "As a practicing Jew and given your interest in Holocaust studies, how on earth do you reconcile being so close with a German?" She was, I correctly surmised, referring to my dear friend and colleague, my brilliant mentor, Dr. William Stefan Lavundi, affectionately called "Willi" by family and close friends. Though admittedly not surprised by the implications of what was a clearly rhetorical and blatantly judgmental statement, I wanted to shout, "You have no idea who he is and where he has been!" Then, his was not my story to tell; instead, I quietly replied, "Some innocent Germans were also Hitler's victims."

One day over lunch at a local pub, I casually asked Willi how he became so fluent in German, French, Russian, and Serbo-Croatian, among other languages. He told me that his mastery of other tongues was born out of necessity from growing up in a multiethnic and multilingual state under various European occupations. That was the first time, too, that he shared painful memories of his shattered childhood, seeing family and friends disappear during the expulsion and annihilation of ethnic Germans of Yugoslavian citizenship by Tito's Partisans beginning in the year 1944. "My family and extended family lost over 20 people—grandparents, uncles, and cousins—who died in the camps established by the Communists who took over Yugoslavia. We were Yugsolav citizens, but our nationality was German, and our people had been in the northern part of Yugoslavia for over 300 years."

When introducing Willi at a college event where he was speaking on the high culture of prewar Berlin, I said that knowing him as I did was akin to getting a doctorate in life. "Great people," he would tell me, quoting Goethe, "talk about ideas. Average people talk about things. Small people talk about other people." Indeed, we would spend hours talking about ideas, everything from philosophy, history, and religion, to art, music, and literature. After Willi was diagnosed with Leukemia and unable to continue teaching, I would visit him at the home of his life partner and soul mate, Philomena. We examined select passages from the epochal classic of Hindu spirituality, *The Bhagavad Gita*. We discussed Andrew De Mello's *Last Meditations,* Josephus' *Antiquities of the Jews,* and the poetry and prose of Goethe. Willi seemed an endless reservoir of scholarly information and insights, oft times humorous, into human nature. Perhaps the best piece of advice I ever received was, "Know who you are. Be who you are. Work on not needing approval from anyone. Then you will be able to live." Words I live by to this day.

Willi was born in 1937 to Emil Lavundi and Maria Theresia Lavundi (nee Karl) in the Batschka countryside of Palanka, an enchanting landscape along the bank where the Danube River flows by mighty castles, Baroque palaces, and monasteries. According to the Apatin Baptism Registry, his great grandparents were from Apatin in Western Batschka. His grandfather Ferdinand and German grandmother Amalia eventually would move from Apatin to nearby Croatia. Willi was the first Lavundi to call Palanka his birthplace.

At the time of his birth, most of the Germans in the Danube region were farmers, craftsmen, factory owners, or merchants. Emil owned a successful knitting machine manufacturing company. The Lavundis shared the large home owned by the Karl Family, Maria Theresia's parents. In the fall of 1944, when Willi turned seven, Josip

Broz, known as Tito, seized power in Yugoslovia, of which Batschka Palanka was a part.

More than 60 years ago, the German Nazi regime committed atrocities against innocent civilians: Jews, Russians, Poles, Serbs, and other people throughout Central and Eastern Europe. At war's end, when combat had ceased and peace supposedly reigned, innocent ethnic Germans, in turn, also fell victim to Adolf Hitler's crimes against humanity. The Donauschwaben, descendants of those Swabians who had sojourned eastward in search of a better life, would now become unwilling scapegoats of the resurgent governments who had suffered under the Fuhrer. German-speaking citizens with only a tenuous link, or really no link at all, to "German-ness" either were expelled or executed using tactics as barbaric as those used by the former Nazi leaders.

Too, as Richard Evans asserts in *In Hitler's Shadow*, the expulsions were also a means of defusing ethnic antagonism and reshaping the demographic profile of Europe according to their own preferences. Much like, one may conclude, their governments' prewar ambition to create ethnically-homogenous nation-states.

During the bloody carnage under the Communist regime, Willi and his parents were imprisoned for six months. His parents later were rearrested and spent two years in the Communist prisons of Knicanin and Pozarevac in Palanka; using the excuse that Emil's machinery came from Germany, the Communists falsely accused him of collaboration with the German government. "It is difficult to talk about when someone close is taken from you. Our only crime was being in the wrong place at the wrong time; our mother tongue was German, Hitler's homeland was Germany, and we were living in Tito's country. The choice was to embrace Communism or Nazism. That is not a choice."

Between 1944 and 1948, the Danube Swabians in the Pannonian Lowlands were all but eradicated. They were deprived of citizenship, lost their human rights, and had their property confiscated. Thousands were tortured and beaten. Many were executed or mutilated. Of those thrown into local concentration or work camps, 65,000 perished from starvation, maltreatment, and disease, and some 15,000 "disappeared." Men and women were sent to forced labor in Russia. Women were raped. In the course of the flight and expulsion of 15 million ethnic Germans, two million perished.

Reflecting on his Palankan relatives, friends, and neighbors who died , Willi admitted, "I feel fortunate that am not numbered among them. Not only were innocent lives savagely taken, but so was our ancestral homeland and identity."

Those who escaped or managed to survive Tito's reign of terror sought refuge in the Western world. Like tens of thousands of ethnic Germans between 1940 and the1950s, the Lavundis fled their homeland in 1956, eventually coming to America and settling in a modest German neighborhood in Northeast Philadelphia. "Under Tito's government I was a slave. Now I was a free man." Speaking little English, the first thing Willi did was flawlessly master yet another tongue. After receiving U.S. citizenship in 1962, he volunteered to join the U.S. Army, where he honorably served his new homeland for six years.

Willi went on to earn a bachelor's degree in literature from La Salle University in Philadelphia, where he would later teach Central and Eastern European Studies. After receiving his master's degree, he served as professor of Comparative Cultural Studies at Schiller International University in Heidelberg. In 1970, he joined the faculty at Ocean County College in Toms River, and four years later received a Ph.D. in German literature from the University of Massachusetts at Amherst. A believer in the importance of international education for students, he founded the College Consortium for International Studies and collaborated with numerous universities abroad. During his career at Ocean County College, Willi initiated partnerships with his alma mater Schiller University and X'ian University in China. He established top tier study programs for students throughout the US in Germany, China, and Israel. Professor Emeritus, Shakespearean and Goethe scholar, and Old World gentleman, Willi truly embodied the spirit of Renaissance humanism.

An innocent victim of exile and imprisonment, Willi triumphed over adversity. His parallel journey of rediscovery, educational and professional achievement, love for his new country, and simultaneous pride in his own cultural identity honors the very spirit of immigration in America.

After fighting a long and valiant battle against Leukemia, Willi passed away peacefully in May of 2010. It was at his memorial mass in Philadelphia that I first met the woman he so cherished, and about whom I had heard such wonderful stories: Katharina Marx, his beloved "Aunt Kathe," whom Willi lovingly referred to as the family genealogist and chronicler of Palankan history.

Today at a spry 84 years old, she still recalls in incredible detail the years she spent in her hometown in the Batschka region, growing up in the same house as Willi. After speaking with her for just a few hours, I knew her story needed to be told. It is but one of many stories about assaults on humanity and man's infinite capacity for evil. It is also a testimony to the resilience of the human spirit, which enabled a young girl to sustain her courage and faith in the face of pure evil.

When I first began my background research, I wondered why there was a disturbing veil of silence surrounding the annihilation of the ethnic German population in the Batschka region. There are, to be sure, many required Holocaust and genocide education programs in place across the country. Here in New Jersey, former Governor Christine Todd Whitman signed legislation in 1994 mandating the inclusion of Holocaust and genocide instruction in elementary and secondary schools. Why then is the ethnic cleansing, the genocide of Danube Swabians, not mentioned in history textbooks or even taught in schools?

Ironically, these ethnic Germans were not tied directly to a true homeland in Germany. While they had some sense of belonging to a larger German speaking cultural group in Europe, they saw themselves as German speaking inhabitants with strong local and regional identities to the places where they and their ancestors had lived for centuries. During World War II, their ethnicity unfairly marked them as Nazi sympathizers despite their noncombatant status. These hard working and G-d fearing people would find themselves on the wrong side of every border as a wave of anti-German sentiment legitimized their persecution and eradication.

As defined by the system of international law established after World War II, (see *Teaching Guide*) the genocide of the Danube Swabians bears striking similarities to that of the Armenians and Volga Germans. During the *Aghed,* the Armenian Genocide during World War I, Ottoman Turkey slaughtered more than one million Armenians and expelled the rest. It has been only recently that the *Aghed* has been included in genocide education programs. The *Russlanddeutsche,* or Volga Germans, were ethnic Germans living along the River Volga in the region of Southern European Russia around Saratov and to the south.

Like their Danube brethren and recruited as immigrants to Russia in the eighteenth century, they were allowed to maintain German culture, language, traditions, and churches. Their genocide encompassed 34 years (1915-1949) under three different rulers: Tsar Nicholas II, Lenin, and Stalin, whose forced dispersal of virtually the entire German population of the USSR to special settlements and labor army work sites during the 1940s brought the total death toll up to around one million. After the Nazi invasion of the Soviet Union in 1941 during World War II, the Soviet government considered the Volga Germans potential collaborators. Cursed as traitors and spies, they were transported wholesale to labor camps, where many died. This final phase of what was called a "resettlement," but was in fact an extermination, permanently destroyed the century-old German communities of the Volga, Ukraine, Crimea, and Caucasus.

The common factor, it appears, driving all of the atrocities that occurred on European soil in modern civilized times, is emotion; all were fired by fear, hatred (both current and ancient), rage, and resentment. The magnitude of the catastrophes and the broad violations of human rights reflect the decimation of human constraints that are accentuated during disruptions of war or modernization.

Today, history books record what is posited as Europe's deadliest wars since World War II: The 1990s' civil wars that erupted in the Balkans, the so called Power Keg of Eastern Europe, with the accompanying horrific war crimes and ethnic cleansing resulting from the complex and bitter conflicts between the Serbs, Croats, and Kosovo, and later between various factions in Bosnia. Today, in 2012, Ratko Mladic, the former Bosnian Serbian leader, is on trial at the Hague for the Srebrenica massacre of 8,000 Muslims. It is tragically ironic that the term "ethnic cleansing" is a literal translation of the Serbo-Croatian phrase, *etnicko ciscenje*, which was employed widely in the 90s to describe the torture and mistreatment of civilian groups in those Yugoslavian conflicts.

However, lest the world forget or ignore, the outbreak of ethnic savagery had happened 50 years earlier to the over 500,000 Danube Swabians living in the national territory of the former Kingdom of Yugoslavia in the Western Banat, the Batschka, Syrmia, Croatia, the Baranja Triangle, as well as in Slovenia on Austria's border.

What is clear is that this watershed event cannot be shrugged off to the euphemism of displacement or romantic notions of liberation. One fundamental condition that made mass ethnic expulsions and disregard for fundamental human rights possible was the assumption that nations had the right to carry out such atrocities in the name of national interest or national security. The primary impetus for the ethnic cleansing was, according to Alfred de Zayas, a revenge against the despised German minorities based on skewed notions of collective guilt and punishment for Nazi atrocities; that the ethnic Germans who had lived for centuries outside of the Reich had collaborated with and benefitted from the Nazis. Shocked by the Nazi war crimes that had come to light, the world looked away, and the "cleansing" of the Danube Swabians, covered by the silence of the big powers, remained without sanction.

Despite all indications that this is a much neglected area of study, there does exist a corpus of scholarly material on crimes against humanity in the Batschka region. This is primarily due to the diligence of Danube Swabian academics and historians, and the tireless commitment of Donauschwaben organizations throughout the U.S. and world to create an awareness of and compassion for what happened to perhaps the last large group of Hitler's victims. Indeed, in Hitler's eyes, the German people had failed the Fuhrer's belief in their destiny for mastery over Europe, and thus, they did not deserve to live.

The German-Jewish philosopher and literary critic, Walter Benjamin, posits that history usually is interpreted by the victors, but it is when the events are interpreted by the victims that history is redeemed. Indeed, the path to truth lies *not* in cold facts or statistics. It is through the eyewitness accounts— the letters, diaries, journals, and memoirs of those who experienced the terror and grief. However inadequate words are, human language is all we have to reach across barriers to understanding.

This, then, is the story of the Donauschwaben. In history and memory.

Ali Botein Furrevig
July 7, 2012

PART ONE

The Donauschwaban: Hitler's Last Victims

There are no nations; there is only humanity. And if we don't come to understand that soon, there will be no nations because there will be no humanity.

Isaac Asimov (1920-1992)

Author's Note: Chapters Two and Three focus on the so-called "ethnic Germans," the Donauschwaben, who lived in the Danube River region under various foreign dominations from earliest times through the post-WWII years. While the history of the German colonists and their descendants in the Batschka area of the Pannonian Lowlands certainly cannot be isolated from events in world history, these chapters should not be read or evaluated as a comprehensive history of WWII or of the Vojvodina areas during those tumultuous times. It is intended, rather, to serve as a cohesive logical narrative and broad framework for understanding the precarious situation of the Danube Swabians living in the Batschka region (particularly in the district of Palanka), as well as the socio-political factors that ultimately led to their expulsion and genocide after WWII.

CHAPTER ONE

Call It What It Is

They fell that year before a cruel foe.
They had little to give but their lives and their passion,
And their longing to live in their way, in their fashion,
So their harvest can thrive and their children can grow.
They fell like flies, their eyes still full of sound—
Like a dove its flight— in the path of rifle
That fell down where it might, that holds on with its might.
As if death were a trifle,
And to bring to an end a life barely begun.
And I am of that race who die in unknown places
Who perished in their pride, Whose blood in rivers ran,
In agony and fright, with courage on their faces
They went in to the night, that waits for every man.
They fell like tears and never knew what for,
In that summer of strife of massacre and war.
Their only crime was life; Their only guilt was feeling.
The children of Armenia, nothing less nothing more.

They Fell: The Children of Armenia by Charles Aznavour (1924-)

"Until the Second World War," said British Prime Minister Winston Churchill, "genocide was a crime without a name."
The man who coined the term in the post-WWII era, placed it in a global-historical context, and demanded intervention and remedial action was a Polish-Jewish jurist, a refugee from Nazi-occupied Europe named Raphael Lemkin (1900-59). His lengthy book, *Axis Rule in Occupied Europe,* applied the concept to campaigns of genocide underway in Lemkin's native Poland and elsewhere in the Nazi-occupied territories. He then waged a successful campaign to per-

suade the new United Nations to draft a convention against genocide, another successful campaign to obtain the required number of
signatures, and yet another to secure the necessary national ratifica-
tions.

Lemkin's conviction that genocide needed to be confronted,
whatever the context, was endorsed resoundingly with the United
Nation's Genocide Convention (UNCG) of 1948, which provided a
detailed and quite technical definition of genocide as follows: [1]

> Article I. The Contracting Parties confirm that genocide,
> whether committed in time of peace or in time of war, is a
> crime under international law which the undertake to pre-
> vent and to punish.
>
> Article II. In the present Convention, genocide means any of
> the following acts committed with intent to destroy, in whole
> or in part, a national, ethnical, racial or religious group, as
> such:
>
> (a) Killing members of the group;
>
> (b) Causing serious bodily or mental harm to members of
> the group;
>
> (c) Deliberately inflicting on the group conditions of life
> calculated to bring
> about its physical destruction in whole or in part;
>
> (d) Imposing measures intended to prevent births within
> the group;
>
> (e) Forcibly transferring children of the group to another
> group.
>
> Article III. The following acts shall be punishable:
>
> (a) Genocide;
>
> (b) Conspiracy to commit genocide;
>
> (c) Direct and public incitement to commit genocide;
>
> (d) Attempt to commit genocide;
>
> (e) Complicity in genocide.

Lemkin also coined the term **ethnocide** as a synonym for genocide. The word was subsequently employed by the French ethnologist Robert Jaulin in *La paix blanche: Introduction à l'ethnocide* to describe patterns of cultural genocide, in other words, the destruction of a group's cultural, linguistic, and existential underpinnings, without necessarily killing members of the group.[2] The term has been used mostly with reference to indigenous peoples to emphasize that their "destruction" as a group involved more than simply the murder of group members.

Between the 1950s and the 1980s, the term "genocide" languished almost unused by scholars. A handful of legal commentaries appeared for a specialized audience. In 1975, Vahakn Dadrian's article *A Typology of Genocide* sparked renewed interest in a comparative framing.[3] It was bolstered by Irving Louis Horowitz's *Genocide: State Power and Mass Murder* (1976), and foundationally by Leo Kuper's *Genocide: Its Political Use in the Twentieth Century* (1981) and his subsequent volume *The Prevention of Genocide* (1985). Kuper's studies were the most significant texts on genocide since Lemkin's in the 1940s and in which Kuper posits: "I shall follow the definition of genocide given in the [UN] Convention. This is not to say that I agree with the definition. On the contrary, I believe a major omission to be in the exclusion of political groups from the list of groups protected. In the contemporary world, political differences are at the very least as significant a basis for massacre and annihilation as racial, national, ethnic or religious differences." [4]

To capture the diversity of early literature on genocide studies literature is impossible in this short section. Suffice to say, Kuper's work was followed by edited volumes and solo publications drawing upon intensive research and offering varying interpretations of the UN definition:

Peter Drost (1959): "Genocide is the deliberate destruction of physical life of individual human beings by reason of their membership of any human collectivity as such." [5]

Vahakn Dadrian (1975):"Genocide is the successful attempt by a dominant group, vested with formal authority and/or with preponderant access to the overall resources of power, to reduce by coercion or lethal violence the number of a minority group whose ultimate extermination is held desirable and useful and whose respective vulnerability is a major factor contributing to the decision for genocide." [6]

Irving Louis Horowitz (1976): Destruction of innocent people by a state bureaucratic apparatus . . . Genocide represents a systematic effort over time to liquidate a national population, usually a minority . . . [and] functions as a fundamental political policy to assure conformity and participation of the citizenry." [7]

Jack Nusan Porter (1982): "Genocide is the deliberate destruction, in whole or in part, by a government or its agents, of a racial, sexual, religious, tribal or political minority. It can involve not only mass murder, but also starvation, forced deportation, and political, economic and biological subjugation. Genocide involves three major components: ideology, technology, and bureaucracy/organization." [8]

John L. Thompson and Gail A. Quets (1987): "Genocide is the extent of destruction of a social collectivity by whatever agents, with whatever intentions, by purposive actions which fall outside the recognized conventions of legitimate warfare." [9]

Isidor Wallimann and Michael N. Dobkowski (1987): "Genocide is the deliberate, organized destruction, in whole or in large part, of racial or ethnic groups by a government or its agents. It can involve not only mass murder, but also forced deportation, ethnic cleansing, systematic rape, and economic and biological subjugation." [10]

Henry Huttenbach (1988): "Genocide is any act that puts the very existence of a group in jeopardy." [11]

Helen Fein (1992):"Genocide is a series of purposeful actions by a perpetrator(s) to destroy a collectivity through mass or selective murders of group members and suppressing the biological and social reproduction of the collectivity. This can be accomplished through the imposed proscription or restriction of reproduction of group members, increasing infant mortality, and breaking the linkage between reproduction and socialization of children in the family or group of origin. The perpetrator may represent the state of the victim, another state, or another collectivity." [12]

Helen Fein (1993):"Genocide is sustained purposeful action by a perpetrator to physically destroy a collectivity directly or indirectly, through interdiction of the biological and social reproduction of group members, sustained regardless of the surrender or lack of threat offered by the victim." [13]

Frank Chalk and Kurt Jonassohn (1990):"Genocide is a form of one-sided mass killing in which a state or other authority intends to destroy a group, as that group and membership in it are defined by the perpetrator." [14]

Steven T. Katz (1994):"[Genocide is] the actualization of the intent, however successfully carried out, to murder in its totality any national, ethnic, racial, religious, political, social, gender or economic group, as these groups are defined by the perpetrator, by whatever means deemed necessary." [15]

Kuper, in his seminal 1983 text, points out that "though the word is new, the concept is ancient." [16] Indeed, the spirit of the term can be traced back to early civilizations. Ben Kiernan, a Yale scholar, has labeled the destruction of Carthage at the end of the Third Punic War (149—146 BC) "The First Genocide." The Mongol horsemen of Temüjin and Genghis Khan in the Third Century were genocidal killers (*génocidaires*) who were known to kill whole nations, leaving nothing but empty ruins and bones. Other examples of crimes against humanity in early civilizations include the genocide of the Anasazi civilization in the American Southwest (800 AD), and the massacre committed by Xue Rengui (614—683) against the Tiele people. [17] To quote Will Durant's famous line referring to the 636 Islamic campaign against Hinduism: "The Islamic conquest of India is probably the bloodiest story in history." [18]

During a 1996 briefing to the U.S. State Department, Gregory Stanton, the president of an organization called Genocide Watch, presented a paper defining the various stages of genocides.[19] Below are the eight stages the organization recognized with their corresponding characteristics:

Stage 1: Classification—Occurs when people are divided into "us and them."

Stage 2: Symbolization—When symbols along with hatred are forced upon an unwilling group.

Stage 3: Dehumanization—When one group denies the humanity of the other group by calling them animals or a disease.

Stage 4: Organization—Special armies or militias usually organized a genocide.

Stage 5: Polarization—Occurs when hate groups start broadcasting polarizing propaganda material.

Stage 6: Preparation—This occurs when people are identified and separated out because of their ethnic or religious identity.

Stage 7: Extermination—Occurs when hate groups begin killing their victims because they do not believe their victims are fully human.

Stage 8: Denial—The hate groups or perpetrators believe that they have not done anything wrong when they are put on trial for their crimes.

The term **Holocaust** comes from the Greek word, *Holokausten*, meaning a sacrifice by fire. It specifically refers to the systematic, bureaucratic, state-sponsored persecution of approximately six million Jews and other groups perceived as "racially inferior" by the Nazis who came to power in Germany in January 1933 and believed that the Germans were "racially superior." Also targeted for annihilation were the Roma (gypsies), the disabled, and some of the Slavic people. Other groups were persecuted because of political, ideological, and behavioral grounds, among them Communists, Socialists, Jehovah's Witnesses, and homosexuals. This massacre of millions became the paradigm case of genocide and underlies the word's origin.

Yehuda Bauer (1984) distinguishes between genocide and holocaust, both of which have the same intent, but "[Holocaust is] the planned physical annihilation, for ideological or pseudo-religious reasons, of all the members of a national, ethnic, or racial group." [20]

Other terms become entwined with genocide and holocaust. **Expulsion** is the forced removal of a population deemed alien or disloyal to the state in order to create a homogenous social entity. Expulsion can be a component of ethnic cleansing and genocide.

While genocide was a term coined in 1943, the term "ethnic cleansing" caught on as an English phrase in the 1990s as a euphemism for ethnic killing or ethnocide through deportation or forcible displacement of people who are undesirable because of their national and/or religious identity, or because of the language they speak. Ethnic cleansing sometimes involves the removal of all physical vestiges of the targeted group through the destruction of monuments, cemeteries, and houses of worship. Ethnic cleansings can be associated with other policies designed to disempower and discriminate against targeted populations, in some instances being associated with mass killings, rape, and torture. In extreme instances, such as that of the Danube Swabians, these policies shade into genocides.

CHAPTER TWO

The Resettlement of Ethnic Germans: Eleventh-Nineteenth Centuries

In Swabia did thy princely father reign
Beloved and all did glad allegiance yield;
And of the people, many now remain
Who fought beneath thy banners in the field.
Sure memory cannot be in Swabia dead.
Towards Swabia let us then our footsteps turn,
And as we the Black Forest's mazes tread,
Reviving hopes will in our bosoms burn.

Johann Ludwig Uhland (1787-1862)

The Danube (Donau in German) River is more than twice as long as any other river in Europe, a silver thread delicately winding through seven countries—Germany, Austria, Czechoslovakia, Hungary, Serbia, Bulgaria, and Romania—on its 1,776—mile journey from Germany's Black Forest Region to the Black Sea. A unifying symbol of hope and inspiration, the Danube's "flood harmonizes every discord and nationality and its spirit is the spirit of pan-Europe," writes Irish scholar and Gypsy folklore expert Walter Starkie in his 1933 memoir, *Raggle-Taggle: Adventures with a Fiddle in Hungary and Roumania*. In retrospect, the haunting and tragically ironic words were penned 15 years before the Danube River region, once a peaceful storyland home to generations of diverse ethnic groups that had settled there 300 years before, would later flow with the blood of the twentieth century Donauschwaben living there.

MEDIEVAL GERMAN AND AUSTRIAN SWABIANS

The Swabian or *Schwaben* historic region of Southwest Germany located in South Baden-Wurttemberg and Southwest Bavaria was bounded on the east by Upper Bavaria, in the west by France, and in the south by Switzerland and Austria, its landscape the mountain range of the Swabian Jura and the valleys of both the Danube River, which rises there, and the upper Neckar River. First settled in the third century by the Germanic *Suebi* and *Alemanni* during the great migrations, the region was one of the five basic duchies of medieval Germany in the ninth century. A country rich in history and with a treasury of German architecture, the duchy was, in 1079, bestowed on the house of Hohenstaufen. Upon the extinction of that dynasty in 1268, Swabia broke up into small ecclesiastic lordships among the various domains of the Habsburg Monarchy in Austria. [1]

Few royal houses proved to be as successful in creating and sustaining an empire as the House of Habsburg, centered around modern Austria. It was Europe's most powerful royal family and a multinational empire in Central Europe that supplied the continent with a nearly uninterrupted stream of rulers for more than six hundred years, from the election of Rudolf of Habsburg as King of Germany and the Holy Roman Empire in 1273, to the dissolution of the monarchy in 1918. When Rudolf conquered Austria, he established that country as the family's new home. Austria, as well as Bohemia, Germany, Hungary, and Spain, were among the European domains ruled by the house of Habsburg. [2]

Swabian pioneer settlement in the Balkan region and Central Europe occurred gradually over many centuries after the eleventh century and in response to numerous political and historical stimuli. In the eleventh century, the area was populated by Hungarian and Serbs. As early as the twelfth century, Swabian miners and merchants were invited by the monarchy to settle in Hungary, and German colonies were peppered throughout the Carpathian Mountains and in Transylvania. However, full-scale German immigration into Hungary and the lands that formerly comprised Yugoslavia—especially

Slovenia, Croatia, Serbia, and Bosnia-were not significant until some 500 years later, and then in mostly the Batschka and Banat regions. The appellations ethnic Germans, *Volksdeutsche, Donauschwaben*, Danube Swabians, and Swabians all refer to the descendants of those Southwestern Germans and Austrians who settled in the Danube region in the late seventeenth and eighteenth centuries following the liberation of Hungary from Turkish rule.

AVARS, BULGARS, AND MAGYARS IN THE BATSCHKA

The largest settlement of ethnic Germans in the Carpathian Basin were in the Batschka region, which had a history, as evidenced by archeological finds, dating back to Neolithic times. Its original inhabitants (Pannonii, sometimes called *Paeonii* by the Greeks) were an Illyrian tribe. From the third or fourth century BCE, it was invaded by various Celtic tribes who originated around the Alps in Central Europe and eventually migrated to Western Europe and the Danube Valley.

With the expansion of the Roman Empire in the first century BC, provinces were established in the geographically strategic Pannonian Lowlands and Batschka district to ensure military security against the incursions of Germanic tribes. The Romans largely regarded the Danube River as their northern frontier, but in the second and third centuries their authority was extended northward into Dacia, in what is now Western Romania. By the first century CE, a substantial Dacian state threatened Roman command of the Danube. The extension of the Dacian state and Dacian raids across the river into Moesia prompted Emperor Trajan in the first decade of the second century to march into Dacia, obliterate the Dacian state and Dacian society, and establish a Roman colony that lasted until barbarian incursions forced a withdrawal back across the Danube, beginning in 271. [3]

The abandonment of Dacia in the second half of the third century was a symptom of Rome's decline. The fifth century marked the end of rule by the empire and the beginning of a period of great migrations from the steppe lands of Asia. The procession of nomadic tribes, many attracted to the opulence of the empire, invaded and ransacked their way to the Eastern Roman Empire, passing through the Batschka district and leaving a path of devastation.

The first invaders were the legendary Huns, warriors who inspired almost unparalleled fear throughout Europe. Called the "Scourge of God" [*flagellum dei*] by the Romans, Attila the Hun was king and general of the Hun Empire from 433 to 453. The Huns were amazing archers and horsemen, and their ferocious charges and unpredictable retreats coupled with their strategic movements brought them overwhelming victories. In 434, East Roman Emperor Theodosius II offered Attila 660 pounds of gold annually with hopes of securing an everlasting peace with the Huns. This peace, however, was not long lived. In 441, Attila's Huns attacked the Eastern Roman Empire. In 447, he launched a second attack on the East Roman Empire. The Roman army was defeated, and the Huns, now left unopposed, rampaged through the Batschka region in 452, after a stay of 10 years. [4]

Following the short Hunnic rule, the area between the Danube and Tisza was inhabited by Germanic tribes, the *Sciri* and *Gepidae*. At the beginning of the sixth century, Germanic *Langobardians* (or Lombards), arriving from around the river Elbe, settled down in the Batschka, but after the appearance of the semi-nomadic Avars, they moved on to Italy. [5]

The Avars, a rapacious and formidable tribe of Inner and Central Asian origin who posed continual threats to Central and Western Europe, settled down in the Carpathian Basin area as early as 568. Their downfall was hastened by the development of the legendary Charlemagne's Frankish Empire, who tried to reconstitute a new vision of empire. Their armies clashed in a fierce war of attrition that lasted seven years, from 796 to 803 A.D. After their defeat by Frankish troops, most Avar tribes returned to the slopes of the Caucasian Mountains. Some others, however, remained and mingled with the Slavs of the area and later with the Magyars. [6]

Also populating the Batschka region at the time were the Bulgars, a Turkish tribe of Central Asia. The Bulgars were living under the sovereignty of the Danube-Bulgarian state until 895, when the Magyars invaded the middle basin of the Danube River. The Magyars had lived in the Black Sea area until they were attacked by the Petchenegs, an Asian Turkish tribe. Under their leader, Arpad, the Magyars defeated the Bulgar Czar Simeon I, but with the help of the Pechenegs, Simeon forced them into Hungary, where they permanently settled around 895. [7]

The term Magyar and Hungarian are identical, but in non-Hungarian languages, the word is used frequently to distinguish the Hungarian-speaking population. Though some scholars believe that there is an ancestral commonality between the Avars and Early Magyars, others posit that their connection is at best tenuous. There is, however, a connection between the Magyars and Huns, which Hungarians have known since time immemorial. Surprisingly, Hungarians are proud of their origin despite the bad reputation given to the Huns and their leader Atilla, who is described in Western history books as cruel and ruthless, with one notable exception. The famous German *Nibelungen-Lied* mentions him thus: "There was a mighty king in the land of the Huns whose goodness and wisdom had no equal."

In the mid-thirteenth century, the Mongols, a powerful tribe who had dwelled in the steppes of Mongolia in Asia, broke through into Eastern Europe themselves, conquering nearly everything in sight. They passed through the Batschka in their flight, pillaging much of the already ravaged area. [8]

OTTOMAN TURKS IN THE BATSCHKA: FIFTEENTH CENTURY

The history of the birth of the Ottoman Empire is also the history of the death of Byzantium, or more correctly, the Eastern Roman Empire. Throughout this period, this ancient and once glorious empire was reduced to a fraction of its previous land area, and it was almost constantly in turmoil as various factions within it fought for dominance. The Ottoman state rose to become a world empire, which lasted from the late-thirteenth century to 1923. Like that of the Habsburgs, its eventual rival, the Ottoman Empire was dynastic; its territories and character owed little to national, ethnic, or religious boundaries, and were determined by the military and administrative power of the dynasty at any particular time. The Ottomans attempted to bring as much territory as possible into the Islamic fold. The non-Muslims living in these areas then were absorbed into the empire as protected subjects. From the late-fourteenth century to around 1700, the armies of the Ottoman Turks, marching under the banner of the Prophet Mohammed, conquered and occupied a good part of the Danube Valley, along with much of Balkan Christendom. The Ottomans took firm control of the Batschka in 1543; this was to last until 1687. Under Ottoman policy, many Serbs were newly settled in the northern places of the Batschka. [9]

The task of resisting the Turks and the religion with which they became synonymous fell by default to the devoutly Catholic Habsburgs, the Austrian dynasty which itself was assembling a Central European empire and thus, Ottoman expansion threatened both the Habsburgs' faith and the complex of lands that gave them claim to political power in Europe. For most of that period, the Habsburgs were frequently at war with them. They struggled against Turkish rule in the Balkans and resisted the Islamization of Europe. Since the fifteenth century, the Ottoman Empire had seen its formerly lucrative East-West trade dry up with the advent of Spanish and Portuguese expeditions across the Atlantic and Indian Oceans. At the same time, scores of years of harmful farming practices only had worsened and in 1683, the Habsburg Empire began to take advantage of the much-weakened status of the Ottoman Empire. [10]

The victory of the Hungarian Imperial Army, under Prince Eugen, was instrumental in gaining a stronghold and pushing back Turkish forces at a surprise attack against the Turks at the Battle of the Tisza. With the subsequent defeat of the Turkish armies at the Battle of Kahlenberg in 1683, Hungarians finally were liberated from

160 years of Turkish rule, and their victory marked the return to the Habsburg Monarchy. [11]

But the frontier steppe lands of Hungary had been decimated and incinerated during the wars against the Muslim invasion, leaving previous agricultural centers in ruin, including the Danube River region, which now was devastated and depopulated. To reconstruct the region, the government carried out a large-scale European settlement project to repopulate and make the war-torn country agriculturally productive again.

There were many provocations for the Habsburg government sponsorship of ethnic German immigration into the empire and what would later become Yugoslavia. It ultimately would strengthen the monopoly of the German economic and political elite. Encouraging immigration into those areas was a means of militia defense against feared Ottoman aggression. The monarchy also wanted to further the Roman Catholic religion in Eastern Europe.

Thus, they encouraged and subsidized the immigration of German farmers and entrepreneurs from the predominantly Catholic states of Southern Germany. Most of these German immigrants originated in the regions of Baden, Schwaben, Wurtenburg, Bavaria, Luxenburg, and Alsace in France. Upon settlement, the German families were given safe passage to protected agricultural lands with auspicious tax exemptions and incentives, free livestock, equipment and seeds, and housing. The Banat and Batschka were the most settled provinces. [12]

BATSCHKA- PALANKA

There were essentially three peak periods of migration or *Schwabenzuge* (Swabian treks) to the now Hungarian owned region: 1723-1726 under the reign of Monarch Karl VI, 1764-1771 under Empress Maria Theresa, and 1782-1787 under Maria Theresa's son , Emperor Joseph II.

When the first group of German colonists set foot on Batschka ground, there already existed a colony of Serbs who had fled from the Turks in the north. The Germans who had travelled westward by horse and wagon and numbered around 120,000 were mostly poor peasants who had farmed the lands of feudal lords. Arriving at the region bordered by the Rivers Tisza and Maros, they did not find the promised land touted by the monarchy; rather, they were confronted by wilderness, dense forests, isolation, primitive living conditions, and marauders. They endured harsh living conditions in uncultivated marshy terrain covered with reeds and cane. Many perished from the plague and swamp fever. Others experienced famine. Some were killed in Turkish raids. Few lived to see the fruits of their labors. [13]

The second group of about 75,000 German colonists also arriving by horse and wagon had to build and rebuild settlements and cultivate the land. They succeeded in reestablishing towns, but their lives, too, were far from easy. [14]

The third group of approximately 30,000 colonists came from the western part of the Holy Roman Empire of Germany and Austria. Since no roads connected Central Europe to the Eastern portion, they journeyed hundreds of miles from Ulm, down the Danube on "little Ulmer boxes," or Danube barges, to homesteads and farming communities in the Batschka. [15]

HUNGARIAN BATSCHKA DONAUSCHWABEN: SEVENTEENTH-EIGHTEENTH CENTURIES

In total, over 125,000 immigrants from the German and Austrian areas came to the Danube area, settling within the Hungarian boundaries. They came from various areas and spoke different dialects, but they were of Swabian origin and thus are historically referred to as Danube Swabians, or *Donauschwaben*. They possessed a pioneer spirit, strong work ethic, stamina, and strength of will.

With the German immigrants enjoying exorbitant government subsidies and now a sizable minority in the significant urban centers, the disproportionate ethnic rights of the Austrian Germans were extended to the new German immigrants. As a result, the

Danube Swabians became quite wealthy and politically influential despite being a small ethnic minority.

It should be noted that the initial immigration to Southern Hungary was driven by Habsburg economic rehabilitation and security considerations and not by German Nationalist expansion. In truth, the German settlers themselves remained indifferent towards German Nationalism into the twentieth century. The loyalty of the Swabians went unconditionally to the Habsburgs.

Under the Habsburgs, German replaced Latin as the official language of Hungary, and German influence became very strong in the cities. Most German settler villages and cities developed a very Germanic architectural and cultural appearance, while the commercial and cultural language of towns settled by German minorities rapidly shifted from Slavic ones to German. These factors were sources of enduring inter-ethnic tensions, as Slavs and Hungarians increasingly rallied for self-determination against the Germans. So too, in areas primarily populated by Orthodox Serbs or Calvinist Hungarians, the presence of Catholic priests and churches became synonymous with what was perceived as the encroaching presence of German imperialism. Adding to the resentment was that in the country, German peasants were the better farmers, and in the cities, many of the master craftsmen such as millers, tailors, shoemakers, masons, and other artisans were German. Throughout Hungary, Swabians held many positions in government offices. [16]

The Hungarian nobility wished to counteract the Swabian influence by making Magyar (Hungarian) the official language of the country, and supported scholars in the development of Magyar literature. Religion, too, was a source of conflict, since the Habsburgs wanted to advance the Roman Catholic religion in a country that had been predominantly Protestant (Lutheran, Calvinist and Unitarian). [17]

The Habsburg Emperor Joseph II, who also ruled as King of Hungary from 1780 to 1790, attempted to reduce friction between Catholics and Protestants by passing the "Patent of Toleration" in

1781. His decree extended to the Jews in Austria as well. He also introduced other reforms with the intent of improving life for the peasantry by removing them from the jurisdiction of feudal nobility, and by taxing the nobles to increase Hungary's share in supporting the cost of government. After Joseph's death, many of his reforms were reversed, and Magyars began to assert greater authority. [18] By the end of the eighteenth century, Hungary was a polyglot nation occupying over 109,000 square miles in Central and Eastern Europe. The population of more than 18 million was 49% Hungarian (Magyar), 17% Romanian, 13% German, 13% Slovak, 4% Serbo-Croatian, and 4% from other ethnic groups. [19]

Since the formation of the dual monarchy of Austria-Hungary in 1867 under the Habsburg ruler, Franz Joseph, the Swabian peasants of the Batschka and Banat provinces contributed to the thriving agricultural economy of the region. They had drained swamps and constructed dikes along the river to help protect the land against flooding. They had prodigiously cultivated and increased the prosperity of the Hungarian farmland. Land ownership was necessary for making a good living in agriculture, and the Swabian Germans practiced the inheritance custom known as *Ahn-Erbrecht* (ancestor inheritance right), in which land holdings were inherited by the first-born son, keeping farm sizes large and intact. Other sons were forced to earn a livelihood as landless farm workers, or in other professions. This custom differed from the Magyar practice of dividing farm lands among their sons, which resulted in increasingly small parcels with each subsequent generation. [20]

The Swabians were faithful and loyal citizens of Hungary, and their national consciousness was quiescent as far as ideologies and political activities were concerned. They lived peaceably side by side with their Serbian, Croatian, Hungarian, Jewish, and Romanian neighbors. While they maintained their own traditions, they also assimilated, learning the languages of their new countries so that they could live and work in a multi-linguistic and multiethnic region. However, they never stopped cherishing and celebrating their own cultural heritage; at home they spoke their mother tongue, read German newspapers, and built and maintained their own churches and schools, which taught in German. [21]

By the end of the eighteenth century, these peaceful and industrious Christian families and their descendants impressively turned the neglected wasteland of the former Ottoman Empire into rich, fertile soil. Using traditional farming practices such as crop rotation helped their new homeland to flourish economically and socially. They grew sugar beets, hemp, wheat, and corn. They kept horses, cattle, pigs, chickens, and geese. Their gardens produced grapes, vegetables, and fruits. What was once useless farmland in the Turkish wilderness would eventually become known as the "Breadbasket of Europe," inspiring Swabian poet Stefan Augsburger to write of his countrymen, "*Nicht mit dem Schwert, mit der Pflugschar erobert, Kinder des Friedens, Helden der Arbeit*" ("Conquered not by the sword, but by the plow, children of peace, heroes of labor"). [22]

What eventually developed for the settlers in the Danube Plains was an entirely new culture; as the centuries turned over, new generations found themselves referring to themselves not as Danube Swabians, but as Yugoslavians or Hungarians or Serbo-Croatians. But the middle of the twentieth century would soon redefine them all, and this new generation residing in the Plains where their ancestors had settled hundreds of years before would be forced to see themselves, perhaps for the first time, as Germans. And soon, as Franz Schmidt points out, they would become scapegoats for having an ancestry that dated back over some 200 years to a country most of them never even had seen.

CHAPTER THREE

When the Danube Flowed Red

Danube so blue, so bright and blue,
through vale and field you flow so calm, our Vienna greets you,
your silver stream through all the lands you merry the heart with
your beautiful shores.
Far from the Black Forest you hurry to the sea giving your blessing
to everything.
Eastward you flow, welcoming your brothers,
A picture of peace for all time! Old castles looking down from high
greet you smiling from their steep and craggy hilltops,
and the mountains' vistas mirror in your dancing waves.
The mermaids from the riverbed, whispering as you flow by,
are heard by everything under the blue sky above.
The noise of your passing is a song from old times
and with the brightest sounds your song leads you ever on.
Stop your tides at Vienna, it loves you so much!
Whenever you might look you will find nowhere like Vienna!
Here pours a full chest the charms of happy wishes,
and heartfelt German wishes are flown away on your waters.

> *Blue Danube Waltz*-Music by Johann Strauss
> Lyrics by Franz von Gernerth

WORLD WAR I: BATSCHKA DANUBE SWABIANS IN THE FIRST KINGDOM OF YUGOSLAVIA (KINGDOM OF SERBS, CROATS, AND SLOVENES)

Prior to World War I, the Batschka was one of several districts belonging to the Austrian Hungarian Empire of the Habsburgs. Following the 1914 assassination of Crown Prince Franz Ferdinand by Serbian Nationalists at Sarajevo, Austria-Hungary declared war on Serbia, signaling the start of the war. The Habsburg rule in

Hungary, which began in 1527, had lasted nearly four hundred years. The loyalty of the Swabians always had been to the Habsburgs, who were responsible for freeing the Danube region lands from the Ottoman Empire and organizing the successful resettlement program. Now, with the collapse of the dual monarchy after its defeat in the war, the ethnic and geopolitical situation, as well as the nationality status of the ethnic Germans of Hungary would change cataclysmically.

At the 1919 Paris (Versailles) Peace Conference, despite the pleas from a delegation of Danube Swabians for autonomy and keeping their homeland undivided, and disregarding President Woodrow Wilson's proclamation of self-determination, the *Donauschwaben* community of 1.5 million was dismantled and distributed among the three successor nations of Hungary, Romania, and The First Kingdom of Yugoslavia, which had been formed in 1918 under the name The Kingdom of Serbs, Croats and Slovenes. Though these nations pledged to provide international guarantees for their ethnic minorities, they were never adhered to by the Serbs. [1]

Thus, following the signing of the 1920 Treaty of Trianon, and without even moving, the Swabian villagers whose families had lived in Habsburg Hungary's Vojvodina (West Banat, Baranja, and Batschka) for nearly two hundred years, found themselves in three different countries separated from one another by artificial boundaries. The majority of the Danube Swabians, including those in Palanka, their mother tongue German, were now involuntary Yugoslav national citizens.

Ethnic conflict and animosity from the majority population towards the Danube Swabians festered following World War I, and this did not bode well for them. The Serbs and the Germans both had been minorities under Hungarian administration. Their relationship drastically changed when the Yugoslav state was formed and the Germans were suddenly a minority within a Serb-dominated state. In the 1920s, while the Swabians did not suffer oppression or subjugation, they were faced with several legal setbacks, including the curtailment of property rights and nationalization of German schools. [2]

Aside from the Danube Swabians' minority status in the Serbian-dominated state, there was the glaring problem of inordinately wealthy ethnic German landowners and a poor Slavic peasant majority. The higher station of the Swabians meant that they were particularly affected by government incursions against the nobility. Making matters worse, the leading position of Germany in the domination of the Yugoslavia, as well as their perceived close affiliation with the Yugoslav Swabians, would contribute to the ethnic Germans' universal identification as a criminal group by vengeance-seeking Socialists after the war. [3]

Too, as a minority, an ethnic entity, and a people, it was difficult for the Danube Swabians to find their common identity. For some 250 years in the former countries of Austria-Hungary, they peacefully coexisted with Hungarians, Romanians, Croats, Slavs, Slovenians, Jews, and other minorities. They not only withstood attempts at Magyarization and Slavicization, but they took even more pride in their national bonds and their ability to live and work with other cultures while still maintaining their own language, social customs, and mores. After all, they had adapted remarkably to political transitions since their settlement in the region in the eighteenth century. Setbacks, it seemed, only strengthened cohesion among the Swabians. [4]

Though they could not reverse the restrictions of the Belgrade school policy forbidding a German-speaking high school, and despite the Serbian disregard for the conditions of the Treaty of Versailles, the minority Swabian population successfully improved their school system. In 1931, the Teachers College was founded. They established a German-language press that published over 30 periodicals and magazines of their own, as well as a daily newspaper, the *Deutsches Volksblatt*. [5]

They also formed their own organizations and representative organs to encourage the development of the culture of the German population: the German Party (*Partei der Deutschen*) and the *Schwäbisch-Deutscher Kulturbund* (Swabian German Culture

Association). The *Kulturbund,* founded by Johann Keks, Stefan Kraft, Peter Heinrich, and Georg Grassel, would be identified after the war by the Communists as a criminal organization, and all of its members (most of the German population) were thereby excoriated as pro-Nazi traitors. Although the *Kulturbund* eventually became a vehicle for National Socialism (Nazism), it initially began as a moderate, integrated German cultural association. The movement did *not* call for a discord from Yugoslavia, a union with Germany, or advocate any violence. Using the mantra *"Staatstreu und Volkstreu"* (Loyalty to the State and Loyalty to the [German] People), the *Kulturbund* promoted the representation of the German ethnic identity, but in active cooperation with its neighbors. [6]

Generally speaking, however, the period between the wars did not significantly alter the lives of Germans residing in rural villages. Their geographic isolation made them less affected by political concerns than those living in cities. Living as they were outside of the Reich, they generally were unconcerned about German Nationalism. And so, despite their balkanized situation, and up until 1929, the small Swabian settlements flourished, and the collective term *Donauschwaben* was widely accepted. Life went on much as it had before the war. The people still spoke their German dialect and kept the culture of their ancestors alive. It would be the rise of Adolph Hitler in Germany and the outbreak of the Second World War in 1939 that would awaken them to a stark awareness of their problematic status as ethnic Germans.

WORLD WAR II BREAKS OUT

In 1933, when the National Socialist (Nazi) regime was established in Germany, the Donauschwaben were one of more than 12 million ethnic Germans living in Central and Eastern Europe outside the borders of the German Reich. The struggle for self-determination of those three million Swabians scattered throughout Romania, Yugoslavia, Russia, and Hungary, "the German question," as Sunic refers to it in *Titoism and Dissidence*, was one of the primary factors contributing to the outbreak of World War II.

While some Danube Swabians embraced Nazi ideology, the rhetoric of German superiority, which preached the total annihilation of non-Aryans, was not accepted and did not go unchallenged. As practicing Catholics (who themselves were frequent targets of the hate speech), the Swabians resisted the Nazi's exclusionary oratory, which could not be reconciled with their theology. Concurrently, the Nazi regime in Berlin viewed the Germans in the Danube region—whom they referred to as *Volksdeutsche*—as existing solely for the political exploitation of the Third Reich. [7]

The first Yugoslavia that was established in 1919 was, much like the pre-World War I Austrian Empire, a multiethnic and multilingual territorial nation of some 14 million people. In 1929, King Alexander had assumed absolute power in Yugoslavia, dissolving parliament and banning all political parties. Ante Pavelic established the *Ustasa*, a Croatian independence movement, in January 1929, and King Alexander I proclaimed the *Kingdom of Yugoslavia* nine months later, creating the term "Yugoslavia," which was used colloquially for decades, even before the country was formed. [8]

On the eve of World War II, Yugoslavia included nearly six million Serbs, about three million Croats, more than a million Slovenes, some two million Bosnian Muslims and ethnic Albanians, approximately half a million ethnic Germans, and another half million ethnic Hungarians. Over the centuries, there had been little love lost among those who now made up Yugoslavia. Adding to the problems to come, Yugoslavia sided with the Allied forces, while Hungary and Romania initially were aligned with Germany. [9]

Yugoslavia had lurched from crisis to crisis. King Alexander I was assassinated in 1932 by a member of the *Internal Macedonian Revolutionary Organization* in Marseilles, France. Prince Paul formed a regency council to govern the country for King Alexander I's young son, Peter II. Parliamentary elections were held in May of 1935, and Milan Stojadinovic of the *Yugoslav Radical Union* formed a government as prime minister that June. Parliamentary elections were held in December of 1938, and the YRU won 54 percent of the vote. Dragisa Cvetkovic formed a government as prime minister in February 1939, but was later deposed in a rebellion led by Dusan Simovic in March of 1941. By March of 1941, their geopolitical position became precarious. [10]

On April 6, 1941, Adolf Hitler gave the order for German forces-backed by Italian, Romanian, Hungarian and Bulgarian Axis allies-to invade both the Banat region of Yugoslavia and Greece. He launched the attack in order to secure Germany's Balkan flank for an invasion of the Soviet Union in a massive assault code named Operation Barbarosa. The attack on Yugoslavia was swift and brutal, an act of terror resulting in the death of 17,000 civilians, the largest number of civilian casualties in a single day since the start of the war. Making the slaughter all the worse was that nearby towns and villages had emptied out into the capital city to celebrate Palm Sunday. All of Yugoslavia's airfields also were bombed, destroying most of its 600 aircraft while still on the ground. On April 17, the decimated Yugoslavian troops surrendered to German troops. Germany and Italy declared that Yugoslavia had ceased to be a nation due to its unconditional surrender, even though the banished king, who with his government in exile had fled to London, claimed the continuation of his country's existence.

As planned, and on June 22, 1941, Adolf Hitler launched Operation Barbarosa. Hitler's intention was always to invade the Soviet Union. It was, along with the destruction of the Jews, fundamental to his core objectives. Following the German attack on Russia, Yugoslav Partisans began raids on ethnic German settlements. [11]

Meanwhile, Yugoslavia was divided up among its various German-allied neighbors. Croatia became a Nazi-allied puppet state headed by Ante Pavelic, leader of the Ustasha extreme Nationalist terror movement. Once again, the Danube Swabians were split up: The Banat remained with Serbia under German military occupation, and Syrmia and Slavonia were attached to Croatia. [12]

Once again, Batschka was part of Hungary. It was beyond the Danube Swabians' political understanding that they could, therefore, ever be considered traitors to the kingdom. After all, throughout the centuries they had been exemplary Hungarian citizens. In addition to making Hungary a world leader in agriculture, they provided the country with world-renowned doctors, composers, artists, engineers, and mathematicians. During the war, Yugoslavia had sided with the Allies while Hungary joined with Germany. The governments of Hungary and the Third Reich signed an agreement giving the Danube Swabians the option of joining the Hungarian or German Army. Most opted for the German forces because of their common language and culture, and because life as a common Hungarian soldier was extremely difficult.[13] That decision would prove deadly because after the war, they would be labeled as traitors.

As the end of the Second World War was imminent, Communism was rapidly advancing into Central Europe. Russian troops passing through Yugoslavia would be followed closely by Tito's Partisans. This eventually would seal the fate of the Danube Swabians who remained in the Banat and Batschka and did not have time to flee the Communist onslaught and their insidious hatred for anything German. Even though the Donauschwaben neither radicalized nor responded to Nazi overtures, they nonetheless would be viewed with suspicion and loathing by Yugoslavian authorities.

FESTERING HATRED TOWARDS DANUBE SWABIANS

Once one of the most privileged groups within the domain of East Central Europe, the Danube Swabians would be perceived after the war as having been supportive of Germany's imperial ambitions in Eastern Europe and would become inextricably linked with war crimes in the minds of many Yugoslavians. And retribution would be brutal.

The hatred toward the ethnic Germans stemmed from, among other flawed reasons, the skewed perception of their relationship to the Waffen SS. In the summer of 1942, there was an unofficial conscription for the Waffen SS. Very few *Volksdeutsche* volunteered due to a number of factors, not the least of which was anti-Reich sentiments. Since its inception, the Waffen SS had operated in the Balkans against the Serbians and Greek Partisans with the usual SS methods. Its activities turned the non-German population of this territory hostile to the *Volksdeutsche*. [14]

However, even if the majority of Swabians were not pro-Nazi in their convictions, the very fact that they didn't turn against the Third Reich despite the exploitation they too had suffered at German hands, seemed to the Serbians to justify the hostility against them. Certainly from Tito's perspective a few years later, this was even more fodder to link the Danube Swabians with the Third Reich and unleash his horrific retaliation. Because of the anti-Serbian actions of the Hungarian military, the Serbs later would ask Tito for permission to take revenge upon the Hungarians. The ethnic Germans who played no role in the military massacres also were included in the Serbian revenge massacres. In the summer of 1942, the first Palankan victim was assassinated by Serbian Partisans. He was Franz Georg Eisenhut, the founder of the Merkur Leather Ware Factory and the son of the internationally-acclaimed artist Franz Eisenhut, who was born in German Palanka in 1857. [15]

The rationale and arguments used to justify the unleashing of a grand-scale genocide against the Danube Swabians is tragically flawed. It is undeniable that the Third Reich committed and either encouraged or apathetically allowed brutal racial genocide, but it is very difficult to accurately assess the degree to which the average ethnic German civilian in occupied Yugoslavia was involved in the atrocities performed by the German Army or other Axis powers. It is probable that a small number of Danube Swabian men supported the Third Reich, given that they would be reluctant to reject the subsidy and support they received from Germany in contrast to the impediment to their cultural franchise they experienced under the Yugoslav Monarchy after 1929. To glean over that is to whitewash history.

Following this fact, it can be concluded that most of the Swabian civilians who actively were involved in criminal activity fled Yugoslavia with the German and Hungarian armies after 1944, meaning that most of those who stayed home in Yugoslavia were loyal to Yugoslavia. Nonetheless, after 1944, the triumphant Socialists universally proscribed the Germans and Hungarians with collective guilt and with uniformly cooperating with the invading Fascists.

Quite simply, it is uncertain in historiography as to what percentage of the Swabian population was involved in the Axis war crimes that would warrant their experience of persecution by the Yugoslavs after the war. It is a moot point, since the Socialists under Tito would resolve this question by universally criminalizing the German ethnic identity altogether.

Too, that only men were allowed to join the SS meant that most of the women and children who were forced into prison camps or expelled by the Socialists after the war were innocent of any direct involvement in wartime atrocities, not to mention the uncertain number of men with political ideologies opposed to Nazism or those who grew increasingly rejecting of the brutality of the German Army in Yugoslavia by the end of the war.

After the war, the Yugoslav Socialists justified the proscription of the Yugoslav Germans by accusing them and the *Kulturbund* of a long-standing conspiracy with the Third Reich to orchestrate the invasion of Yugoslavia and subjugate the Slavs under the authority of the Swabian minority. This allegation is presumptuous and largely baseless. As yet, no evidence has been located in historiography to indicate any conspiratorial collusion between the *Kulturbund* or Swabian groups with Nazi Germany prior to the invasion. The *Kulturbund* continuously espoused a program of cooperation and membership *within* Yugoslavia, rather than any call for irredentism or independence.

So too, Yugoslavia and Germany were in close political and economic partnership under the Tripartite Pact. Yugoslavia was highly dependent upon the German economy and German investors; approximately 65% of Yugoslavia's imported products and machinery came from Germany, often at reduced rates. Few Swabians could have predicted that Berlin would obliterate such a positive economic and political union, which was maintained under the Tripartite Pact even until the invasion began. Few Swabians (or even Yugoslavs or Germans) could have foreseen the incredibly impromptu declaration of war on Belgrade by Hitler in response to the monarchy's sudden uncertainty in political behavior. Even after Peter II took power, he ultimately chose to maintain the ties with Germany. [16]

There was insufficient time for the Yugoslav Swabians to plot a long-standing conspiracy with Hitler to destroy Yugoslavia. There was no enduring conspiracy for invasion and genocide against the Yugoslavs between the Swabians and the Third Reich, which the Socialists claimed after the war when they began the imprisonment of the entire German community. Yugoslavia was just as much home to the Swabians as the Germany that their ancestors left some two centuries prior.Seen as Nazi collaborators and out of retaliation for crimes they didn't commit, Donauschwaben civilians and soldiers would become victims of Tito's "Final Solution," what De Zayas coins "a terrible revenge," a barbarous ethnic cleansing campaign that resulted in the carnage and extermination of some two million innocent men, women, and children.

OCCUPATION AND ATROCITIES BY RUSSIAN TROOPS

It is noteworthy that despite the political chaos, until the fall of 1944, German life under Hungarian rule had been tolerable. Now, with the defeat of the German Army and its allies becoming more and more apparent, the German population in the Batschka became increasingly worried about their fate. Many, given the choice to flee the advancing Russian troops or stay, heeded the evacuation call and decided to leave. Over 50% of the ethnic Germans remained. [17] In early October of 1944, when the first Russian troops marched into the Vojvodina, there were at least 200,000 ethnic German civilians in their native land. In those areas, including the Batschka, occupied by Russian troops, the military governments of the Serbian Partisans were quickly installed and were in power until the third of March of the following year. Attempts by their political opponents, other Nationalists and Royalists to share in government were denied, and they eventually were liquidated. During their two month occupation in October and November, the Red Army of the Soviet Union inflicted its own devastation upon the German minority, ostensibly as an act of punishment for Germany's atrocities against Russia during the war, not the least of which was Operation Barbarosa. Russian soldiers ceaselessly tormented citizens and destroyed property, much like what had happened to the Jews during the Russian pogroms in the Pale of Settlement when anti-Semitic sentiments flourished.

Russian soldiers not only arbitrarily mistreated Germans, but also Magyars, loyalist Serbs, and other Slavs. There are disturbing documented personal accounts depicting rampant murders, theft, and acts of rape and sexual abuse committed against the German and Hungarian women whilst Soviet commanders looked the other way. The Red Army also compounded the Yugoslav imprisonment policy by demanding that Yugoslavia participate in the Soviet directive to deport thousands of "pro-Axis" minorities to Russia for forced labor in the quarry mines as part of the reconstruction effort. Many ethnic Germans were deported on the same trains that the Croats and Germans had used to deport Yugoslavia's Jews and other victims to Auschwitz and Croatian death camps. At least 27,000 ethnic Germans in Socialist Yugoslavia were forcibly escorted by the Red Army or the Yugoslavs and shipped to the Ukrainian SSR for compulsory labor. It is estimated that the number of deaths as a result of exhaustion, freezing, malnutrition, and disease is near 10,000. However, the worst was yet to come.[18]

GENOCIDE OF ETHNIC GERMANS BY TITO AND HIS PARTISANS

The civil wars that broke out within Yugoslavia while WW II was winding down pitted three main groups against each other: the Croatian Nazi-allied Utasia; the Communist Partisans led by the Croatian-born Josip Broz Tito; and the Serbian Chetnicks, a pro-monarchy guerrilla group that also eventually collaborated with the Germans and Italians.

The Communists emerged the victors. Since 1937, Tito was the secretary general of the underground Central Committee of the illegal Communist Party of Yugoslavia. Even though Germany and Russia still were considered allies, Josef Broz Tito was disillusioned with the Russians, whom he felt had failed to support the Partisans with promised supplies. So, while he was hiding in Zagreb, surreptitiously receiving messages from Russia, he was also training his secret Partisan army. [19]

In 1941, when the Germans invaded Yugoslavia, Tito made his way to Southern Serbia, where he took control of the resistance movement. He and his movement were very successful and a constant thorn in the side of the Nazis in Yugoslavia. Not even fearful retaliation against the civilian population of Yugoslavia did anything to stop what the Partisans did. Those who were led by him gave him the title "Marshall of Yugoslavia" in November 1943. It was a title that became internationally recognized.

By the time the Nazis were driven out of Yugoslavia, Tito was the undisputed head of state. He had made a name for himself independent of Stalin; he was a Communist, but was now independent from Moscow. With the German occupiers gone, Tito then turned to eliminating domestic rivals, including members of the originally anti-Fascist Chetnicks (who eventually collaborated with the Germans to try to stop Tito) and the fascistic Ustashe, who from the beginning had supported the Nazis as a vassal state in Croatia. Members of both organizations were summarily tried and executed en masse. [20]

Now Tito was almost solely in control of Yugoslavia, and he was free to seek the course that he wished. A policy of ethnic cleansing had already been adopted in 1943 at a conference in Jajce, Bosnia, and was finalized a year later in Belgrade by the Anti-Fascist Council of Liberation for Yugoslavia (AVNOJ). The edict stipulated that ethnic Germans were "enemies of the people," and were to be disenfranchised and stripped of their civil rights, including the right to life. Their farms, factories, businesses, and shops were seized and became the property of the Yugoslavian state. The confiscated property amounted to 97,490 small businesses, factories, shops, farms, and diverse trades. The confiscated real estate and farmland of Yugoslavia's ethnic Germans came to 637,939 *hectares* (or about one million acres). According to a 1982 calculation, the value of the property confiscated from ethnic Germans in Yugoslavia amounted to 15 billion German marks, or about seven billion U.S. dollars. [21]

The proclamation edict at Jajce provided a perverted sense of legality for internment, torture, and massacres. Beginning with the Bloody Autumn of 1944, over 2,000 ethnic Germans died at the hands of the Partisans, and 5,000 perished. Thus began the end of the 400-year Swabian culture, which once had flourished along the pastoral Danube countryside.

The secret police organization, Office for the Protection of the People (OZNA), established by the Communist Party of Yugoslavia, set up regional offices to remove the local leadership and intimidate the people. They arrested many well-known ethnic Germans, especially those holding government seats, all in the name of "political cleansing." Together with the execution commandos of the *Aktion Intelligenzija*, respected members of the community—industrialists, well-off tradespeople, rich farmers, clergy, capitalists, intellectuals, and people accused of being "capitalists" or "counter-revolutionaries"—were targeted, tortured, and executed in the villages. Even though the Catholic Donauschwaben neither radicalized nor responded to the Nazi overtures, they nonetheless were viewed with increasing suspicion by Yugolslav authorities. [22]

All Swabian men in occupied Yugoslavia (and especially the Banat) were compulsorily required to serve the Third Reich in some fashion, either by joining SS-Prinz Eugen, the *Wehrmacht,* or by providing another service. Regardless of their diverse political beliefs and their varied levels of approval for Nazism, Yugoslavia's German civilians were effectively forced to become what Yugoslavs later would identify as traitors and a pro-Fascist irredentist "Fifth Column." Therefore, even when Swabians participated in the SS killing squads, the German minority's level of personal approval of the Nazi occupation or their betrayal of Yugoslavia remained questionable.

Batschka Palanka had a total population of approximately 13,000, half of whom were ethnic Germans. Because they were geographically located at the front line, they were the first to experience the bloodlust of the Partisans. The innocent victims of the beatings and executions perpetrated in October 1944 included young men between 15 and 17 years old, and ninety men who were considered prominent residents of the community. [23]

Later that month, a census to declare one's nationality was taken. The Partisans had lists of German surnames for each house. Young men were taken from their homes, marched barefoot into the snowy forest, and shot after being forced to dig their own graves. In late October, before the internment of each village, the Partisans randomly selected over 200 young men whom they tortured and killed. The same fate awaited the older men in the community, who were forced into boats set adrift in the strong current, where they then were shot at from the land. Some were thrown into the river, where they drowned. Roman Catholic Church leaders were no exception. Among those who were killed in the Danube River was the beloved Priest, Karl Unterreiner. Hungarian-born Joseph Cardinal Mindszenty was imprisoned by the Communists from 1944 to 1945 for speaking out against the Communist regime. [24]

The Partisans were not the only committers of atrocities. There were disturbing spontaneous instances of random citizen groups that engaged in frenzied murders. One tragic incident took place in Palanka, where local gypsies joined a group of Partisans killing prominent Germans, Magyars, and Serbs. [25]

In Palanka, the first internment was November 29, 1944. The Partisan troops in the Batschka regions had strict orders to forcibly suppress the resistant forces and organizations in the villages left behind by the retreating enemy. Most of those holdouts were Germans and Hungarians, who became victims of horrific revenge killings. Armed Partisans barged into homes and gave some residents 10 minutes to pack clothing and provisions for a few days. The Danube Swabians then were herded into an open, rainy field with several thousand others and forced to march 50 kilometers (30 miles) under guard to the town of Pasicevo. Many older people collapsed from exhaustion. [26]

There was pillaging and mass rapes. Children were slaughtered after going through gruesome torture and dismemberment prior to succumbing to death. The ethnic Germans were expelled from their homes and dispossessed throughout Yugoslavia by the Partisans. Close to 150,000 Danube Swabian civilians were imprisoned in numerous labor and-in total-eight large concentration camps that had been built for the elderly and infirm as well as for children under 14 years of age and mothers with little children. On Christmas Day, 1944, over 8,000 women between the ages of 18 and 35, and men between 16 and 35 were shipped in open trains to ancient Russian coal mines. Only half of them would return. [27]

World War II ended in May of 1945. The tragic events that followed pretty much eradicated the Swabian population in the Danube region. Seven hundred thousand Danube Swabians were deprived of their citizenship and had their properties confiscated. Thousands of young men were executed. The rest were thrown into concentration camps, where in the years 1945 to 1949, tens of thousands perished from maltreatment and disease.

Every village had a concentration or internment camp, usually that was set up in homes in evacuated villages. In the Batschka, there were camps at Jarek (7,000 deaths), Gakova (8,500 deaths), and Kruschiwl (3,500 deaths). In the Banat, there was Molin (3,000 deaths), Knicanin (11,000 deaths), and Seidenfabrlk in Syrmisch Mitrovitz (2,000 deaths). In Slavonia, there were camps in Valpovo (1,500 deaths) and Kerndia (1,000 deaths). The camp villages were patrolled by armed guards who were known to be cruel and sadistic. Even though the camps at Gakova and Jarak were set up for those unfit to work, the partially able-bodied prisoners were forced to work in the fields or camp. [28]

In total, 65,000 Danube Swabians perished through hunger, epidemics, and shootings in the labor and concentration camps within three years. Of that figure, 15,000 were never accounted for. It is estimated that thousands of ethnic Germans were tortured and killed. By 1945, over 200,000 ethnic Germans in Yugoslavia became captives of Tito's regime. Through 1948, over 60,000 civilians perished, some from exhaustion as slave laborers, others from typhus, malaria, forced starvation, and malnutrition in concentration camps. About 35,000 succeeded in escaping from the camps across the borders to Hungary and Romania. [29]

Additionally, Tito's Partisans handed over some ethnic Germans to the Red Army, who transported them to Siberia, where they were subjected to working in the mines as slave labor. Frail and debilitated Russian men and women were expelled to Germany or Austria. From 1946 on, approximately 40,000 orphaned Danube Swabian children were sent to Communist children's homes throughout Yugoslavia. They were given Slavic names and underwent radical Slavicization. Through the efforts of the German Red Cross, about 5,000 children eventually were able to be reunited with relatives in the West.

The irony is stunning. No other river in the entire world has inspired so many poets, musicians, and painters. Along no other river can such a tremendous variety of scenery, historic cities, magnificent architecture, and cultural treasures be found. The German poet Friedrich Hölderlin called the Danube a "refreshing, melodious river, sometimes foaming with high spirits, at other times dreaming serenely." The Danube River inspired Richard Strauss to compose his Romantic masterpiece, *The Blue Danube Waltz,* whose sentimental lyrics have become the unofficial Austrian National Anthem. Cruising down the winding Danube today, tourists can enjoy passing through the charming towns, forested hills, and commanding fortresses along its banks. However, for thousands of ethnic Germans, the shadows of that Communist reign of terror and the ghosts of their brethren whose blood once flowed in the river will forever haunt the now serene landscape. Perhaps if you listen closely to the sound of the lapping waves, you can still hear the screams.

CHAPTER FOUR

The Jews of the Batschka

No no: they definitely were
human beings: uniforms, boots.
How to explain? They were created
in the image.
I was a shade.
And he in his mercy left nothing of me that would die.
And I fled to him, rose weightless, blue,
forgiving— I would even say: apologizing—
smoke to omnipotent smoke
without image or likeness.

Testimony by Dan Pagis (1930-1986)

Even though the narrative of Jewish history since biblical times is fraught with diaspora and persecution, it seems remarkable that both the Jewish and ethnic Germans living in the Vojvodina region during and after World War II were innocent victims of Adolph Hitler. Hitler's state-sanctioned propaganda blamed the Jews for Germany's defeat in World War I and for the subsequent economic depression. His hate-filled rhetoric portrayed Jews as evil Communists seeking world domination, and who were, like the Roma, Poles, the mentally and physically disabled, Jehovah's Witnesses, and homosexuals, a biological threat to the pure and superior Aryan race.

Even in Roman times, there was a Jewish presence in the Carpathian Basin. There are also traces of a Jewish population along the banks of the Danube during the tenth century. Benjamin of Tudela, the twelfth-century Jewish traveler and chronicler, mentions the influence of the Jews on the inhabitants of the Balkans.[1]

The Jewish population in what is now Serbia increased greatly following the expulsions of the Sephardic Jews from Spain and Portugal in the fifteenth century. The adjective "Sephardic" and corresponding nouns Sephardi (singular) and Sephardim (plural) are derived from the Hebrew word *Sepharad*, which refers to Spain. The Sephardim made their way east and settled in areas that were part of the Ottoman Empire, where they were welcomed. They prospered during the ensuing centuries, working as merchants and traders in an atmosphere in which, for over 600 years, they would be relatively free from violent persecution or governmental interference. During the period of the Austrian rule over Northern Serbia from 1718 to 1739, the government's attitude toward the Jews was generally good. During the Serbian wars of independence (1804—30), some of the Jews fled from Belgrade.[2]

The second group of Jews to arrive in the region in the eighteenth century were the Aschkenazic Jews, who hailed from France, Germany, and Eastern Europe, and their descendants. The adjective "Ashkenazic" and corresponding nouns, Ashkenazi (singular) and Ashkenazim (plural) are derived from the Hebrew word *Ashkenaz*, which is used to refer to Germany. [3]

Notably, the Jews who settled at this time in neighboring Hungary, under Maria Theresa, were subject to an enforced restrictive Jewish policy. In the Letter Patent of 1743, Jews could settle only if they paid a tolerance tax. Jews eventually were allowed to settle in newly-founded towns in Vojvodina, where economic expansion was occurring. Joseph II promulgated an Edict on Tolerance in 1782 for Hungary, which markedly lessened the restrictions on Jews in the Vojvodina. Jews were allowed into previously excluded economic enterprises, and Jewish schools were allowed. [4]

The most significant Jewish communities, though, were founded in the 1840s. The Jews engaged in commerce and in import-export trade. By the middle of the nineteenth century, the Ashkenazim began moving to towns and cities, earning livings as farmers, merchants, doctors, and veterinarians. The Ashkenazi Jews formed a close-knit insulated community. Their mother tongue was either Hungarian or German. Though they had little contact socially with other nationalities in the German villages, they maintained an amicable and symbiotic business relationship with their Swabian neighbors.

Predominantly grain dealers, the Swabians brought their produce to them and received their money for it. This information is corroborated by Josef Schram, who notes that most of the chroniclers of Batschka German communities refer to the Jews in a positive manner, and there was no enmity between the two groups. Anti-Semitism as an organized movement was non-existent. After World War I, some signs of it appeared, but the situation improved again. The church evinced a favorable attitude toward the Jews. [5]

With the establishment of the Yugoslav Kingdom after the First World War, about a hundred Jewish communities with 70,000 Jews were included in the new state. The Jews generally belonged to the middle class, but there were also some impoverished communities. The Jews were well represented in industry, commerce, and artisan activity. They also held an important place in the banking business. There were some professions, such as the army officers, cadres, the upper government services, and journalism, from which the Jews were almost totally absent. [6]

There were Jewish elementary schools, which had existed before the Yugoslav Kingdom, in the towns of Zrenjanin, Osijek, Sarajevo, Senta, Zagreb, and Zemun. The government prohibited the opening of new elementary schools. In Vojvodina, there were *yeshivot* in Senta, Subotica, Kanjiža, and Ilok. Jewish children attended the general schools, in which two hours weekly were allocated for Jewish religious studies. From 1928 to 1941, there was a seminary in Sarajevo for the training of *akhamim* and teachers on a secondary school level. Among the scholars and authors, mention should be made of Lavoslav Šik, a historian of Yugoslav Jewry, the poet Hinko Gottlieb, and Siegfried Kapper. An important place in Yugoslav literature was held by Isak Samokovlija, a Bosnian novelist who died in 1955. [7]

Before its dismemberment, there were about 80,000 Jews within the entirety of Yugoslavia. There had never been much anti-Semitism in Yugoslavia before World War II. The anti-Semitic sentiments really originated in Croatia and Slavonia. In Croatia, Jews were persecuted as part of a general genocide of foreigners. Jewish property and money were taken away, and by the end of 1941, two-thirds of Croatia's Jews had been imprisoned; many later were killed by the government. The rest were deported to Auschwitz and other concentration camps in Eastern Europe. Some escaped to the Italian Zone of Yugoslavia, and some were rescued and hidden by local citizens. [8]

When Germany-along with Hungary, Italy, and Bulgaria-invaded Yugoslavia in April of 1941, she divided Yugoslavia among its allies, keeping Serbia for herself, including the 16,000 Jews living there. Hitler was hell-bent on ridding the region not only of Jews, but of Serbs. Demonstrating resistance and defiance, Serbia disdainfully rejected Hitler's offers to join the New Order in Europe, and now they would witness Hitler's wrath. There was a price to be paid: total and complete annihilation of the Serbian nation.

Hitler ordered his commanders to be ruthless and merciless towards the Serbian population. Among the victims of this slaughter were 100 Jews. Some of the German officers told their troops that they were taking revenge and executing hostages who themselves did not commit any crimes, but because of the German soldiers killed in the First World War. As De Zayas points out, in the closing phase and aftermath of World War II, the Serbian collective psyche figured strongly in how they dealt with the remaining German minority. [9]

Like in the other countries they invaded, the Nazis immediately began implementing anti-Jewish discriminatory policies, forcing Jews to wear an identifying badge, removing them from professional life, and defining where they would live. Men aged 16-60 were recruited for forced labor, businesses were taken away from Jewish owners, and Jewish banks were blocked. From 1941-1942, most of Serbia's Jews were murdered by mass executions, gas vans, and starvation. Only 1,500 Serbian Jews survived. On the day after the occupation of Belgrade (April 13, 1941), German troops ransacked the Jewish shops. Within a week, the Jews were ordered to register with the police, and eventually 9,145 Jews, out of a total prewar population of about 12,000, were registered.

About 3,500 to 4,000 males from the age of 14 to 60 were forced to clear the buildings that had been razed by the bombardment, while women aged 16 to 40 were given menial tasks in the German military installations. A special police detachment was formed to deal with the Jewish population. A "Jewish Organization" (*Jevrejska Zajednica*) was created to attend to the needs of the Jewish population. The Nazis forced the organization to collect contributions from the Jews and provide hostages to ensure Jewish compliance with their orders.

After the German invasion of Russia, the occupation regime became even harsher. In one incident alone, at the end of July, 120 Jewish hostages were shot to death in the village of Jajinci, near Belgrade. In the Banat, after robbing the Jews of all their property and belongings, the Nazis placed them in camps and a few weeks later deported them to Belgrade, adding another 2,500 people to its destitute Jewish population. By the end of September, all Jewish men aged 16 and above were put into a concentration camp, situated in Topovske Šupe, a Belgrade suburb. [10]

In Yugoslavia's Batschka and Baranja districts, which were now under Hungarian rule, the fate of the Jews (and, to a certain degree, the local Serbs) was no less savage. In Subotica, the main city in Batshcka, 250 persons were killed in the first days of the occupation. [11]

In January of 1942, there was an unprecedented orgy of anti-Serbian and anti-Jewish racism and murders in the city of Novi Sad. The first slaughter took place on the third day of the occupation, when 500 people, both Jews and Serbs, were murdered. Novi Sad had a rich Jewish history. It was founded in 1694 as an Austrian fortress, *Petrovaradin,* built to guard a Danube River bridge from the Turks. In the first decades of the eighteenth century, three Jewish families are known to have lived in Novi Sad, most coming from

Nikolsburg in Moravia. In 1717, a synagogue and cemetery are known to have existed. The Jewish community of Novi Sad was officially established in 1748. A *Hevrah Kaddisha* was founded in 1729 as a "Holy Welfare Society." A synagogue was built in 1829. A Jewish school in Novi Sad was constructed in 1802. [12]

The Jewish community of Novi Sad was initially under the leadership of a rabbi, then by a judge. In the nineteenth century, a president was appointed. The Jewish community was restricted and rigidly controlled by the municipal government of Novi Sad, which supervised the elections of rabbis, teachers, and other Jewish political and religious leaders. There was also a split between the upper-class, wealthy Jewish merchants and traders, such as the Hirschl family, which had dominated the community for over a century, and poorer Jews who sought autonomy for the community and no government oversight. [13]

During the inter-war years, from 1918 to 1941, Novi Sad Jews played a prominent role in the economic, political, cultural, and social life of Novi Sad, which belonged to Yugoslavia. They were prominent in publishing and journalism. In 1935, the Jewish Cultural Center in Novi Sad was constructed, which contained a kosher delicatessen, theater, and facilities and offices for sports, humanitarian, and cultural societies. There was a Jewish newspaper, and Zionist organizations were established. [14]

Now in the last days of a bitter cold January in 1942, Hungarian troops surrounded and sealed off the city, signaling the *hladni dani* or "cold days" in Novi Sad, the systematic mass murders of Serbs and Jews. The pretext for the raid was a small rebellion that occurred outside the city. A clash between resistance fighters and a Hungarian troop detachment caused the death of four Hungarian soldiers, and in reprisal 1,300 men, women, and children were rounded up and shot to death by Hungarian forces. Serbs and Jews were murdered in the streets.

The Jewish community was threatened with deportation to Croatia unless it made an immediate payment of 50,000,000 *dinars*;

after great efforts, 34,000,000 were raised. Altogether, about 3,500 people were killed in Vojvodina in the initial stage, among them 150—200 Jews. The Hungarian state set up temporary concentration camps in the Batschka and other villages where approximately 2,000 Jews and Serbs spent two weeks to two months. Those who were not sent to the camps were assigned forced labor. Some 2,000 Jews passed through these camps in the first two months of the occupation.[15]

But without question, the most notorious atrocities and murders occurred at the Strand, Novi Sad's beach on the Danube River. On that day, the Danube River was frozen solid with a temperature of -25C. Hungarian forces brought over 1,300 Serbs and Jews—men, women, children—to the frozen Danube River and lined them up in four rows. Hungarian forces then shot them in the back. Holes in the ice were made by the Hungarian troops with shells. The bodies were then thrown into the broken ice of the Danube River. Many of the bloated corpses washed up on the shore, while other corpses flowed down the Danube River to Belgrade. Bodies continued to wash up for two weeks after the atrocity.

In all, over 1,300 people were killed that day. Of those killed, 813 were Vojvodina Jews, 380 were Vojvodina Serbs, 18 were Hungarians, 15 were Russians, 13 were Slovaks, eight were Croats, three were Germans, two were Ruthenians, two were Slovenians, and one was a Muslim. There were 492 men, 418 women, 168 children, and 177 elderly. Seven Serbian Orthodox priests were among those killed along with one Jewish rabbi, 126 salesmen and shopkeepers, 100 tradesmen, and 81 pupils. The end came in March 1944, when Hungary was taken over by German forces. On September 17, a transport of 3,600 Jews from the Bor Mines (where the labor battalions were concentrated) was dispatched in the direction of Belgrade; about 1,300 prisoners were murdered or died en route, and the rest were deported to Germany.

A short while later, a second transport of 2,500 Jews, which included a large contingent of Vojvodina Jews, was organized. The rest of the Jews from Batschka and Baranja were deported on April 25th and 26th, 1944. About 4,000 Jews from the area of Novi Sad were interned at Subotica, while the Jews from the eastern part of Batschka were dispatched to a camp in Baja in Hungary; in May 1944, the group from Subotica also was sent to Baja. Eventually all the inmates of both camps were deported to Auschwitz. In total, 4,620 Vojvodina Serbs and 3,310 Jews were killed. [16]

In 1942, the Hungarians ordered the formation of forced labor battalions into which all Jews and Serbs between the ages of 21 and 48 were drafted. Some 4,000 Jews from Batschka and Baranja were conscripted into the battalions; 1,500 were sent to the Ukraine, near the front, where they succumbed to disease and starvation or were murdered. Only 20 of the entire group survived the ordeal. The others were sent to Hungary and Serbia, where they were put to work in copper mines and on the railroads, together with about 6,000 Hungarian Jews. In spite of the harsh conditions to which they were exposed, they managed to survive for a while.. Some were able to escape, and several hundred were liberated by Tito's Partisans, finding refuge with the population in Serbia and the Banat. Eventually all the inmates of the Baja camp, as well as those of the Batschka Topola camp, were deported to Auschwitz.

All of these massacres and atrocities were orchestrated by both Hungarian and German political and civic leaders. Nonetheless, after the war, Danube Swabians and Croatians were accused of complicity in these crimes against humanity. [17]

Notably, there were about 85 persons in the Vojvodia, many of whom since have obtained "The Certificate of Honour" and "The Medal of the Righteous" from the Yad Vashem Holocaust Museum in Jerusalem for risking their lives to save Jews. In his book, *The Righteous*, Gilbert relates the stories of Mathilda Nitsch and Risto Ristic. In the town of Susack in Croatia, a Roman Catholic woman, Mathilda Nitsch, who owned a boarding house, helped Jews escape. She hid them in her boarding house and stole false passports for them so that they could escape deportation. In the Serb town of

Bijelina, Risto Ristic woke up his Jewish neighbor, Rahela Altara, in the middle of the night to warn her of a pending roundup of Jews. Rahela, her mother, aunt, and siblings fled to a neighbor's house, where they were hidden and supplied with food and necessities from Risto. Eventually, they managed to escape the territory under the control of Tito's Partisans. Risto then warned other neighbors, saving at least 20 Jews from deportation.

Cardinal Archbishop of Zagreb, Alojzije Stepinac, condemned Croatian atrocities against both Serbs and Jews and himself saved hundreds of Jews during the war by both direct action or secret rescripts to the clergymen, including mixed marriages, false birth certificates, and conversion to Catholicism. As early as 1936, Stepinac supported Jewish refugees from Germany and Austria in Croatia. In 1938, he founded Action for Help to Refugees. In a confidential rescript to Croatian clergy in 1941, Stepinac wrote: "The role and task of Christians is on the first place to save people. When this time of madness and wildness is over, only those will remain in our Church who converted out of their own conviction, while others, when the danger is over, will return to their faith." [18]

Among the Jews Stepinac would save in 1943 were 60 inmates of the Jewish Old People's Home in Zagreb that the German authorities ordered to leave within 10 days or they would be sent to a German concentration camp. In May of 1943, Stepinac openly criticized the Nazis, and as a result, the Germans and Italians demanded that he be removed from office. Pope Pious XII refused, and warned Stepinac that his life was in danger. In July of 1943, the BBC and the Voice of America began to broadcast Stepinac's sermons and criticism of the Utasha Regime to occupied Europe. At the end of the war, at a mock trial, Stepinac was found guilty of Nazi collaboration and was convicted and sentenced to 16 years' hard labor on October 11, 1946. [19]

In his duties as a chaplain, Adam Berenz temporarily served in Batschka Palanka and Bukin. In September 1922, he was appointed as administrator of the parish of Nova Gajdobra, from where he subsequently was transferred as chaplain, and then administrator of the main parish of Apatin, the West Batschka district. Berenz was arrested because of his involvement as editor in charge of the Catholic weekly paper *Die Donau*. In his columns, he had waged an unyielding resistance for almost a decade against National Socialist neo-heathenism, and against the arrogant, senseless conduct to which National Socialism had given rise.

One night, the word *Volksverräter* (Traitor of the People) was smeared on his front door. The outside wall of the rectory was scratched with swastikas and derisive caricatures. Such methods were used to foment hate against him. At 9:30 PM on May 22, 1944, a little over three months since Hungary had been occupied by the German military, the Gestapo arrested him. He was taken to Sombor in an automobile and locked into a jail cell, from where he was transferred to a Gestapo jail in Szeged a week later. After being "sentenced" for being a resistance fighter against Nazism, he was transferred to the concentration camp in Batschka Topolya, where Jews and Communists were being detained. [20]Archbishop Grosz interceded on his behalf with the Interior Minister of Hungary, and received permission to release Berenz.

Until the day of his arrest by the Gestapo, Berenz fought against National Socialism through his weekly paper and thus documented the resistance movement of the Donauschwaben. He also protested against the thesis of collective guilt, which was attributed to the Donauschwaben after the war.

As beautiful pearls are produced by the suffering of an oyster, so each genocide creates beautiful heroes, not only among the victims and survivors, but also among those who risked their own lives in order to help save the lives of those who were persecuted. Even among the most sorrowful memories, the humanitarian acts performed by compassionate individuals shine above the dark side of brutality.

Today, on the bank of the Danube River in Novi Sad, is a marble memorial chiseled with the chilling but powerful words written in

both Serbian and Hebrew: *As people, we must forgive, but never forget.*
It is a message that applies to the innocent Serbian, Jewish, and
Donauschwaben peoples who were all victims of Hitler's expulsions
and genocidal barbarism. A message that reminds us: Remain
human, even in inhuman circumstances.

Katharina Marx with her parents Emil and Elisabeth (nee Pautz).

Firehouse Tower in Palanka. The Lavundi and Karl families lived towards the end of the block behind the church. Top Right: Main street in Palanka where stores were. Bottom Right: In distance, the Church of Immaculate Conception.

Willi Lavundi with his Aunt Kathe at her Philadelphia home, 2005.

Katharina and Nikolaus Marx at their daughter Christine's marriage to George Telford, 1988.

Donauschwaben Society of Philadelphia's annual "wallfahrt" pilgrimage to honor those lost in the ethnic cleansing

Emil Lavundi and Maria Theresia Karl on their wedding day, Palanka 1937.

Kathe with granddaughters Emily and Rebecca in Palanka, 2009.

Kathe's maternal grandmother, Rozalia Pautz nee Schon 1942. She and her husband perished in Jarek Camp.

1954 at Villach Austria Transit Camp awaiting documents to travel to America. Sitting: Anton and Elisabeth Karl holding Brigitte Griesbach; Standing left to right: Otto Heinrich, Elisabeth Griesbach, Katharina Karl, and Willi Lavundi who was on vacation in Austria.˘

New Palanka home of Kathe's maternal grandparents.

Home of the Lavundi and Marx families in Batschka Palanka.

Kathe and Nikolaus Marx at Philadelphia Donauschwaben Society's Trachtenfest. Kathe is wearing the dress her mother wore in 1912.

Two grandsons of Anton Karl (in back) in Palanka 1942. Willi Lavundi is wearing hat. Otto is holding whip. Emil's workshop can be seen in the background.

Marriage of Elisabeth Karl to Heinrich Griesbach, Palanka 1939.

Marriage of Katharina Karl to Nikolaus Marx, 1957 Philadelphia.

25th anniversary celebration of the Philadelphia Donauschwaben Society, 1982.

Mr. and Mrs. Emil Lavundi celebrate Emil's 70th birthday with grandson Jordan Lavundi.

Map of the Batschka area. Palanka is on bottom left along Danube.

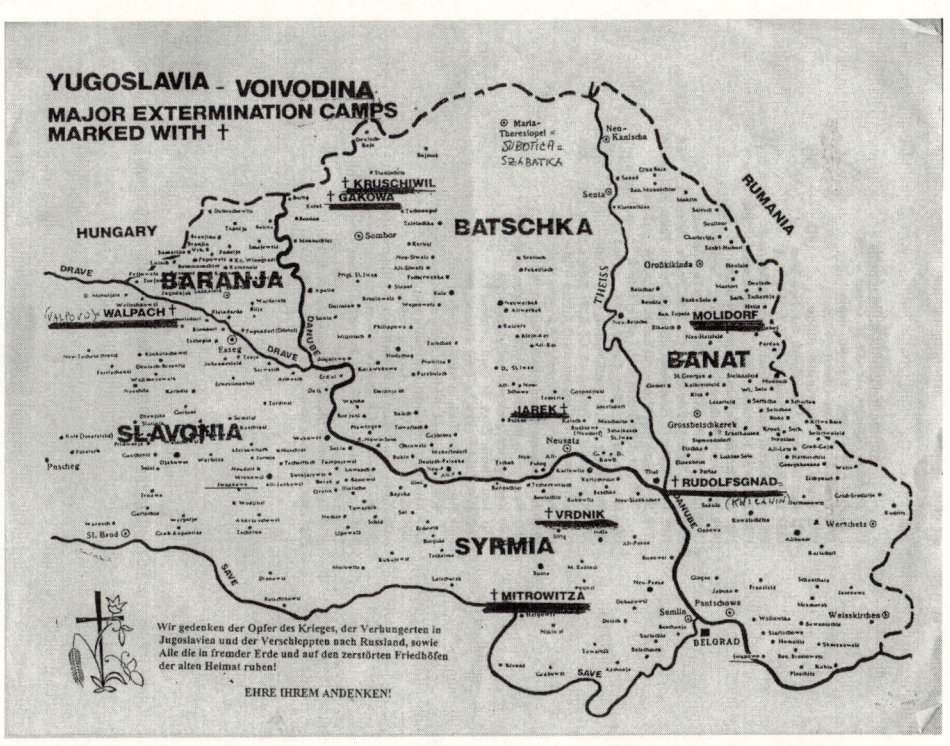

Vojvodina Camps. Extermination camps are marked with cross.

PART TWO

The Katharina Karl Marx Story

I decided to devote my life to telling the story because I felt that having survived, I owed something to the dead, and anyone who does not remember, betrays them again.

Elie Wiesel (1928-)

Author's Note: This section is based on extensive interviews conducted in 2011 and 2012 with Katharina Karl Marx. I have made every attempt to preserve her unique personality, character, and speech in the presentation of the events she describes. The historical facts, places, and people are depicted as accurately as her memory and my own research can attest to.

CHAPTER FIVE

Fields of Sunflowers

Where the Danube turns to the south;
It flows through Pannnonian fields;
Joining with the Theiss, Temesch and Drau;
washing around our flatland cradle;
There a homeland blooms among a riot of flowers
and splendor from the moor arising,
Wrested from wild soil, with bold courage
and Swabian toil, richness from abundant furrows.

Homeland of Danube Swabians so fair!
You were the jewel of the Danube valley.
We carry you in our hearts, our lost holy Grail!

Forgetting, we left for many countries;
where we create and build in honor and toil,
Though we also love our newly adopted homeland,
we faithfully recall the old.

Homeland of Danube Swabians so fair!
You were the jewel of the Danube valley.
We carry you in our hearts, our lost holy Grail!

Our Danube Swabian Song (Rootsweb.com Banat Archive)

Katharina Karl Marx's modest two-story home on a tree-lined street in Northeast Philadelphia is what my mother would call *haimeshe,* a Yiddish term meaning welcoming and homey. It exudes old world charm. Shelves are lined with books in German and English, many about the Danauschwaben and Palanka.

There are framed precious photographs of loved ones long gone hung side by side with pictures of new generations who cannot even imagine life without freedom, dignity, and human rights.

In the small kitchen, Kathe is preparing lunch for us. Instead of my mother's traditional chicken noodle soup with matzo balls, Kathe was cooking turkey broth with farina-based *gries knodel*. Her cabbage, prepared with ground turkey and rice, was reminiscent of my own mother's stuffed cabbage with beef. She had baked German cakes, which she placed alongside the homemade *hamantaschen* I had brought along. When she asked about the significance of this three-cornered fruit-filled pastry, I explained that it is symbolic of our holiday of Purim, celebrating Queen Esther, who saved the Jews of Persia from extermination. At that moment, it struck us both as to how similar our cultures were: tragic stories of dispersion, intolerance, and abuse of power, but stories, too, that can inspire us about the indestructible human spirit and faith. Like the Jews who managed to survive the brutality and unspeakable horrors of the concentration camps, Kathe is determined to honor her heritage and her faith, which helped her survive the hard times, a faith that could not be broken by any regime.

As this was our first interview, I hoped to formulate a chronological framework for our discussions, and suggested to Kathe that she tell me what is was like growing up in Palanka before the Communist deluge, snapshots of her life in happier times. As she stirs the soup, amid the fragrant steam rising from the pot comes a stream of memories, shadowy gray ghosts of departed neighbors and ancestors.

"Come into the living room," she says softly, and there she carefully unfolds a large piece of linen onto the sofa. The aging fabric reveals her meticulously hand-drawn genealogical family tree dating back to the early nineteenth century. She points to the lineage of her grandfather, Johann Karl, who had four children: Johann, Anton, Josef, and Katharine. *My grandfather Johann suffered from asthma but that he lived to be 81 and that he had all of his teeth, which he cleaned daily with salt. My uncle Josef came back from Russia where he was a POW in 1919. My grandfather had been saving money to buy Josef a farm, but all his money that was in government war bonds was lost. My father Anton married in 1912. He was supposed to receive the fields and the new house, but Grandfather decided to give the house to Josef. My mother and father, who now had two young children, had to look for a house and found one less than 100 yards from the church. There was a park in between. Barns and stables had to be built as well as a "chardak," which was a place to store the corn till it dried out. The farm was a good distance from home. There was a house, a "sallasch," on the farmland where the farmhands and their families lived. My grandfather had built our "sallasch," which had a kitchen, two bedrooms, a stable, and a port for the machinery. He was very skilled and was able to build chairs and narrow beds with wood frames. There was a well alongside the house.*

Katherina Karl was born in Batschka Palanka in 1928 to Anton and Elizabeth Karl (nee Pautz) into what she calls, "the most beautiful community in the Southern Batschka on the Danube."

Palanka's history was connected inexorably to the Batschka region of which it was a part. [1] The scenic village was nestled between the Danube and Tisza Rivers, and set against the romantic backdrop of the middle arc below the Carpathian Mountains. Historians and archeologists have proved that people lived in the area for centuries. There are many archaeological objects from Stone Age, Bronze Age, Iron Age and Roman period.

In the eleventh century, this area was populated by Hungarians and Serbs. Backa Palanka is first mentioned as a settlement in 1486, as a suburb of Ilok called Ilocka. Until the sixteenth century, this area was administered by the Kingdom of Hungary. In the beginning of the sixteenth century, the village was in the property of landowner Laurence of Ilok, a duke of Syrmia. It was destroyed by the Ottomans after The Battle of Mohács in 1526, but was then rebuilt as small Ottoman fortress named Palanka. During the Ottoman administration (sixteenth-seventeenth century), Palanka was mostly populated by ethnic Serbs. In 1687, Palanka was included into the Habsburg Monarchy, and more Orthodox Serbs settled here. Palanka was then mentioned as a small town with 167 houses, all of them Serb (1720 census data). Later, Germans, Slovaks, and Hungarians settled here as well. It was part of the Habsburg Military Frontier from 1702 to 1744. Nova Palanka (New Palanka) was founded between 1765 and 1770, two kilometers away from original Palanka (which then became known as Stara Palanka-Old Palanka) and Nemacka Palanka (German Palanka) was founded by Danube Germans in 1783. Those three towns would become one city, Batschka Palanka, in the twentieth century.

Eleven years before and following the dismantling of the Austria-Hungarian Empire in 1918, the Danube Swabian community was parceled out among the three successor nations of Hungary, Czeckoslovakia, Romania, and Yugoslavia. Palanka now belonged to the newly-formed state of Yugoslavia under Alex II, and was made up of the prior kingdoms of Serbia, Croatia, and Slovenia.

By 1928, Palanka was the peaceful homeland to many genera-tions of Swabian, who now numbered 7,500. Kathe's neighbors were all Danube Swabians, but the region also had a population of people of different fatherlands with little in common. There were approxi-mately 4,500 Serbs who practiced Greek Orthodoxy and 1,000 Protestant Slovaks. The town also housed some 200 Jews who were merchants and had their own synagogue in town. Each group formed their own cultural and economic organizations, but *everyone got along. We were not political people; we were peaceful and did not feel it necessary to have weapons. Yes, we lived with the Serbs, but we had our own schools and church, as did the Serbs. I later learned from one of my parent's friends that there was some animosity of the Palankian people towards the local Serbs, who were not perceived to work the land as often or diligently as the Donauschwaben, who secret-ly hoped that the Hungarians would return.*

Kathe gently removes an unpublished German manuscript from the dining room sideboard. We sit together on the stuffed sofa, paging through the bound, typewritten record authored by Dr. Jakob Schmidt explaining how plans for the villages had been laid out in Vienna. The towns generally were built in a square checkerboard pattern, with the Catholic Church and its surrounding square in the center of the town. The style of the buildings was a modified Baroque, and came to be called "settler's Baroque." Each village, however, had slightly different designs for the decorative finishes on the buildings, and the differences still are visible today.

The houses were built perpendicularly to the street, and consisted of a series of adjoining rooms, with the parlor on the end that faced the street, with sheds for domestic animals on the opposite end. Long, covered porchways extended the full length of the house. The Swabians were known for keeping their houses and gardens clean and carefully maintained. Each house plot was surrounded by a fence, and the courtyard within the fence contained grape vines, fruit trees, and the household garden. Hogs were bred, raised on corn, and exported for sales at markets in Vienna and Prague. The streets in the villages were wide, and were used as pathways for community activities, such a baptisms, weddings, and funeral processions. Cattle were also led down the street to the common pasture in the surrounding area of the village. The streets, too, always were kept clean.

The average house lots in Palanka were quite large. Young Katharina Karl, her parents Anton and Elisabeth, along with her sister Maria Theresa, her husband Emil Lavundi, and their young son, Willi, shared the long house. Kathe's sister Elisabeth had married Heinrich Griesbach, and they lived in Ilok with their young son, Otto. Years later, their daughter Brigitte would be born in Austria. Emil's knitting machine manufacturing company was situated in back of the home. There were stables for horses, cows, pigs, and chickens and large vegetable gardens were in the rear of the lots replete with fruit trees and grape vines.

The Karl farm was located near Wekerle, some nine kilometers from the village. Katharina vividly recalls the sprawling farmlands dotted with towering sunflowers. The farms grew mainly wheat, which was sown in autumn, and barley, corn, and hemp, which were sown in spring. Because of the sandy soil in Neu Palanka, there was a considerable amount of fine tobacco harvested until it was forbidden to do so.

Like other victims of a diaspora, though the Danube Swabians had to leave their homeland and treasures behind, they carried with them their memories. Kathe remembers life as a farmer's daughter. She and the other children rose early in the morning. Twelve-hour days were the norm, and even more for the children of farmers. Everyone had a chore to do; the children usually were charged in the spring with gathering *brennessel*, or nettle plant, for the geese. It was very important to bring the harvest home in early October before the rainy season, since there were only mud roads to the town of Wekerle.

If the rain mixed with the mud, there was the danger of the wagon sinking into the ground. That the wagons would sink into. They were bad times for farmers, and my parents had to struggle through the 1930s. Interest was up to 18%; field products were low in price. We also grew hemp. The stems of the hemp were treated in water for 10 days, then broken off with a handmade machine. The fine, platinum-blond strings that were left were like hair. They were bundled and twisted and sent to Germany, where it could be made into ropes, tents, and clothing. The wooden stem remains were used to heat in special heaters filled with small pieces of wood.

It is an uncomfortably hot September afternoon, and so we move outside to the fenced-in rectangular back garden where a welcomed light breeze can be felt. It is a mecca of meticulously maintained fruit trees, herbs, grapevines, rose bushes and colorful beds of sweetly perfumed flowers. Today, there is an abundance of quinces that recently have fallen off the trees. Kathe tells me that this fruit is similar to a pear but much more tart. She fills a basket for me to take home. *They make wonderful preserves,* she smiles, *just make sure you cook them in water with sugar.* She is surely a farmer's daughter.

Kathe shows me photos of the Danube River, the lifeblood of the Palankian people. Fishermen were prosperous because of the abundance of fish in the Danube. *Many of the local fishermen would return to town early in the morning pushing a wheelbarrow filled with fresh fish from the Danube, calling "Fisch Ribe!" and people would come out of their houses to buy the fish, especially on Fridays. Farmers, merchants, and millers also benefitted by the proximity to the river.*

In addition to its agriculture, Palanka was a center of commerce and trade. The majority of the merchants and store keepers were Jewish. The Abels owned a vinegar factory. The Deutsch family ran a paper and book store. There was a millinery shop run by the Goldsteins. A grocery store in town was owned by the Greens. Like most Jews in the Batschka, the business owners left the region before the war and the chaos that ensued under Tito. Several did return to Palanka in 1948 and 1949, only to discover that their homes were neglected and their customers gone. They left the Danubian Plain and went either to Israel, where some of their neighbors already had settled, or to other cities in Yugoslavia, such as Novi Sad. About 30 of the families stayed in Israel, where they had migrated to a decade or so before. Some Danube Swabians ran businesses and workshops. *There were shoemakers who ordered the finest leather from the Loch Co. There was a knitting shop where you could buy sweaters, dresses, hats, and shawls. You could also bring your own material to the local tailor to have a coat, suit, or dress custom made. A seamstress made delicate underwear for dowries. She also made fine dresses like those seen in the fashion magazines from Vienna, Paris, and Berlin.*

A Viennese man owned a *Yutte* factory where many locals were employed to make sacks and tents out of the coarse jute material. There were hemp factories as well that sold products to Germany. There were butchers, flower shops, bike stores, a leather shop, metal shop, cleaners, and grocery stores. There were inns and a few small hotels.

Palanka had doctors who had studied in Vienna and Berlin. *Even though they didn't have many X-rays, they did a great job in removing splints from the eyes of local metal workers. Of course, I remember having a painful root canal from the local dentist who did not use any anesthesia.*

Whether or not the people were pious, the social customs of the village centered around church activities. Sunday dress for the women consisted of the *tracht*, or village costume, which included a distinctive dress plus decorative shawls, scarves and aprons. Each village had its own type of dress and hair style. Baptisms and weddings were joyous and festive events for family and neighbors, and included a street procession and special dinner. Professional pictures were taken at weddings, engagements, and communions. To the Danube Swabians, what symbolized all of life's events from birth to death and all the joyous celebrations in between was rosemary, or *Rosmarein*. This little evergreen shrub with blue flowers was emblematic of love, faith, and the land. It was customary at a baptism that godparents wear a sprig of rosemary on the left lapel or scarf as a sign of their faith. At the baptismal dinner, the table was decorated with rosemary as a symbol of love for the newborn. At name day celebrations, the celebrant received an apple with a sprig of rosemary tucked inside. At a burial, a rosemary bush, a sign of mourning, was planted on the grave, signifying eternal life.

Most of the 7,500 Germans were Catholic, and their lives were intertwined with the church. People attended church services on Sundays and participated in both ecclesiastical and secular events and feasts in the town. Birthdays, Kathe, informs me, were never celebrated; instead, there was name day, the feast of the child's patron saint.

The major feast of the year, *Kirchweih*—the church consecration days—was held on a Sunday in autumn. The young men wore special hats that had been created by the young women of the village, and all took part in a procession led by a selected young couple. The day included a special mass, a festival dinner, and dancing in the street. In the larger cities, where people were craftsmen and shopkeepers, a German middle class and cultural life developed. Here, schools in German areas of the cities also had instruction in German. There were German-language newspapers and magazines. There were concerts, plays, and balls. Temeschburg, Romania, known as "Little Vienna," was famous for its fine German theater events and other cultural activities.

As early as the mid-eighteenth century, notes Palanka historian Niklaus Hepp, a German school already existed when the first colonists arrived. [2] It was taught by a Frenchman from Alsace. As the nineteenth century came to a close, the state took over the school, conducting classes in Hungarian. German was taught as a foreign language. After World War I, the Yugoslav State took over the school, and Serbo-Croatian became the compulsory language. German parallel classes were forbidden, and the German students had to change to the Serbian department or leave school. Palanka had a German high school from 1921-1931. In 1933, parallel classes were restored at the Serbian grammar school. By 1939, a private German grammar school was built.

In 1935, when Kathe attended elementary school, classes were held in a convent. The classes started at 8 AM until 10 or 11 AM. After a lunch break, it was back to school from 2 until 4 PM. Thursdays were a half day, and there was school on Saturday as well. *The classes were taught by the Catholic sisters from Filipow, who taught first grade through fourth in German. In the first two grades, with 40 children in class, students learned three alphabets: Gothic letters, Latin, and Cyril, and could read books in all three. The fifth and sixth grades were taught in Serbian by a German-Serbian teacher, Mrs. Flock. Religion classes were only taught by priests: Fathers Fritz, Johler, Merkl, and Grieser. There was a choir group that would perform concerts and plays.*

Serbian history was taught in the schools. Kathe recalls learning about the 1389 Great Battle of Kosovo, which sealed the fate of Serbian independence. The battle has filled a large place in the historical and literary imagination of the Serbs. The fatal "field of the black birds" has gathered around it a rich garland of heroic ballad poetry and romantic legend, which was first revealed to Western Europe by the German poet Herder in his charming collection, *Stimmen der Volker* (Voices of the Nations). A little later, Goethe, avowedly adopting the version of an Italian priest and traveler, produced a very perfect translation of one of the masterpieces of Serbo-Croatian ballad poetry, *The Wife of Hassan Aga*, and it was this which did much to stimulate interest in the admirable collections published during the twenties and thirties of last century by the Serb philologist Vuk Karadzic. Kathe tells me about the legend of the medieval Serbian hero, Kraljevic Marko. *He was said to be so strong that with one hand, he was able to throw a pair of oxen with a plow at the Turks during Battle of Kosovo. It was also the site where nine Jugovic brothers were killed. According to folklore, the mother of the brothers prayed to G-d to give her the eyes of a falcon and the white wings of a swan so that she could fly to Kosovo and find her family.* The myth was the subject of the poem, *The Death of Mother Jugovic*, where G-d grants her wish but her family already was gone.

Sundays in Palanka began with church in the morning, lunch at noon, and walks afterwards. Kathe recollects Sunday afternoons when young Serbian men and ladies would stroll down to the Danube along the main promenade, shaded by stately horse chestnut trees, stopping along the way to window shop. Others would sit on the benches under the trees, enjoying people watching. *The Serbians were all dark haired and dressed in their Sunday finery. The Serbian girls wore large gold coin necklaces. The more affluent their family, the larger the necklace, in hopes of attracting a potential suitor.*

In the summers, Kathe would help the family with chores, but she also enjoyed trips with friends into the Acacia or Bukin Forests to hear brass bands playing. Every summer up through 1941, before the young men were drafted into the German or Hungarian armies, a dance instructor from Novi Sad would come to Palanka and teach classes at the Klespies Hotel. *It was an amazing event. The dance hall was large and elegant with mirrored walls. We met people from all over Palanka and many first loves and lifelong friendships developed at these classes. When I went back to Palanka in 2009, I found that the hall had burnt to the ground and all that was left were the memories.*

Social activities in Palanka were plentiful year-round. Kathe talks about the dances that were held in the villages at various places determined by demographics. *The farmers' daughters and sons met at the Schmauss-Schumacher Inn, the workers met at Linder, and Dornes and Kleschpies was where the merchants gathered. The Slovaks met at Berner at Prell Corner. The Lapplanders (meaning little house people) in the northern part of town met at Berner. The German population congregated at all of these places. Some evenings, we would all meet to enjoy "Fischpaprikasch," a fish dish, and dancing. There were glorious carnival balls and ecclesiastical events, and feasts.*

The Palanka people took tremendous pride in their renowned and well-equipped fire brigade, founded in 1873 and rebuilt in 1933 opposite the German Palankan Church. The fire brigade also had a famous brass band that played concert music throughout the Batschka region. The village had a sports field, sports clubs, and a library. As did the Serbs and Jews, the Danube Swabian women had a charity organization called *Philantropia* that tended to the elderly, sick, and needy in their villages.

Of much importance to these people of German ancestry was encouraging a national consciousness and sustaining a spiritual and ethnical culture. The Swabian-German Culture Association was instrumental in attaining those goals. To cultivate German music and song, there were the Liederkranz Club and the Choral Society. The latter was called a "watering can club," because wine was served in large containers. There was a Palankan band that played at operettas. The Palanka Casino Club, founded in 1871, also fostered cultural activities such as lectures and theatre performances.

Surrounded by magnificent chestnut trees and cornfields, Palanka seemed an idyllic paradise to those who lived there. Kathe nostalgically talks about the magic and tradition of Christmas Eve in the old country, where every year she, like all children, would look in awe at the secretly decorated and glorious tree glimmering with glass balls, colorfully wrapped salon candies, golden nuts, and small apples—all bathed in the warm light of candles. *The families sang traditional carols, and children were told to be very, very good so that the Khristkindl, the little Christ child, would come to their homes and bring gifts. That evening, the little ones sat on the Ofenbank, a bench, anxiously awaiting the arrival of the Christ child.* There was the tinkle of a door bell. An apparition in white, fully grown, holding a linen sack filled with apples, walnuts, hazelnuts, oranges, and figs. Somehow, this mysterious person knew all about the children's mischievous ways and whether they were attentive to their studies and catechism. The children would promise to try to be even better next year.

Later that evening, the family would tell stories and play games before the tired youngsters were carried off to bed. *The Midnight Mass was the highlight of Christmas. On Christmas Day, the children received gifts of scarves, socks, gloves, and shoes. I went to church services and then visited my godmother, who always had small gifts; usually a gingerbread doll for the girls and a gingerbread horse for the boys. The tree would be dismantled on Holy Three King's Day, January 6th, the same day our Serbian neighbors celebrated Christmas with straw in their homes, symbolizing the birth of the Christ child.*

Palanka, she tells me, welling up, *was surely the most breathtaking place.* Indeed, in 1920, Stuttgart scientist Dr. Hermann Rudiger made an extensive study trip into the Batschka region and writes in his diary about the beauty of Palanka, and of Ilok, which lies directly across the Danube River:

Palanka is by all means the most beautiful place on the Danube River in the whole Batschka Region. The left or northern bank of the river is a considerable distance from the town. A marvelous promenade stretches from the town to a landing spot in the shadow of high chestnut trees along a partly water-soaked embankment. The view on the opposite bank of the Danube is most attractive. Here the lower mountains of the Frusca Gora rise 50 meters above the river and the plain of The Batschka Region. Cloister, church,, castle, and the imposing fortress of

Ilok emerge from the sap green pastures and greet you. Small stream boats transporting vehicles on a ferry [connect] the two river banks. Back and forth there is very frequent traffic because on the hills on the other side there are the vineyards of the people.[3]

For her first 12 years, Kathe's life in the Batschka went on as usual, since the region was not yet significantly impacted by the war raging throughout Europe. Teenagers continued to go to dances and the cinema. There were weddings, celebrations, dances, and festivals. The music would stop in the spring of 1941.

CHAPTER SIX

When the Music Stopped

How I wish I could go back there,
Where such happiness was mine,
Where I lived and where I dreamt through
My youth's year the most divine!

While away I felt the longing
To return to the homeland,
The old bliss, I kept on hoping,
Would still be there close at hand.

Finally good fate and fortune
Brought me to that vale again;
But I found upon returning
That my hope had been in vain.

The old brook was there to greet me
Bouncing sounds from rocks around;
But my good friend's voice was missing,
           Now and Then by Nikolaus Lenau (1802-1850)

It was the spring of 1941. World War II had started in Europe two years earlier, but for the most part, life along the tranquil Danube flowed on for the villagers. Thirteen-year-old Kathe and her friends were celebrating the near completion of their first full year at the Serbian-run high school and looking forward to more carefree days ahead.

The Balkan Campaign in 1941 dramatically and tragically shifted the landscape and history of the region. On Palm Sunday, German and Hungarian troops invaded Yugoslavia. Danube Swabian men and boys were drafted into the Yugoslavian Army. Many of the Palankan town leaders and merchants, including Kathe's uncle Josef Bautz, were taken as hostages across the Danube from Novi Sad to the Peterwardein Fortress. The battle lasted one week, until Easter Sunday, at which time Yugoslavia was split up. The Batschka was officially annexed to Hungary, who had ruled that area up until 1918, and whose president was now Horthy Miklos. Horthy had been an ally and was promised that he would get the area back. The Banat remained with Serbia, but under German military occupation. Syrmia and Slavonia were incorporated with Croatia.

Palankan schools shifted over the centuries as the state authorities changed. From the mid-eighteenth century, when the colonists first settled in the area, there was a German primary school for boys and girls. In 1898, the state took over the private convent-run school and classes were now conducted. Following World War I, the Yugoslav State overtook the school, and Serbo-Croatian became the compulsory language, but the ministry of education permitted German parallel classes for the German Palankans. As Jakob Schmidt notes, that was "a blessing for the German culture there since many Swabian children who had gone to the Hungarian school prior to 1918 had become strangers to their German people." One of the problems, Schmidt asserts, is that the German teachers and education were known to be superior to that of the Serbian schools, which led to ill feelings towards the Germans. In December of 1931, with the new public school law, German parallel classes no longer were allowed, and German pupils either had to attend the Serbian classes or leave school. Kathe had been schooled under the Serbians until 1941.

Now, Serbian schools were run by Hungarian teachers in the mother tongue. Kathe and her friends would have the arduous task of not only learning about a new culture, but mastering a foreign language they had had little exposure to, having been born after the fall of the Austria- Hungarian Empire. It was, Kathe admits, *a difficult challenge, but it truly is a beautiful language. We learned about the*

Hungarian hero Toldi Miklos, and studied the exquisite poetry of Petofi Sandor and Arany Janos. It was also required that students wear a navy hat with the Hungarian crown and logo.

Hungary, in hopes of reclaiming lost territories from the Communists, sided with Germany in the war. An agreement signed by the German Reich gave Hungary's German soldiers (now Hungarian citizens) the option of being drafted into the Hungarian army or joining the German battle group. Because of ethnic, linguistic, and cultural connections, most opted to join the German troops. *We were technically not German citizens, and they technically had no right to draft our people, but they did, and those men served until the end of the war, or the end of their lives. After the war, we would be accused by the Communists of being traitors.* Some of the Swabians served involuntarily in field units of the Waffen SS, which was made up of a majority of Bosnian Muslims. Kathe explains that *there are no records of war crime trials of ethnic Germans of Yugoslavia serving in the Waffen SS.* I delicately question her about the presence of Nazis in the town. *The term Nazi was not known or ever used. We never saw Nazi SS troops. We were a simple, peaceful, hardworking people. What most of us wanted was to be able to claim our German heritage, to have German schools. Even today, many older Germans do not have a correct understanding of German spelling, having been schooled in Hungarian.*

Kathe's older sister, Elisabeth, and her husband Heinrich Griesbach lived in Ilok across the Danube River. *It was a very beautiful view from our side of the Danube. The hills of Fruska Gora rose about 50 meters above the river and were famous for their plush vineyards. There was a ferry that ran between the two towns and which cost three dinar. We would visit Elisabeth and my nephew Otto, but from 1941-1944, because Ilok was part of Croatia and Palanka part of Hungary, you needed a passport to cross the river. Ilok was often attacked during the night by the Partisans killing people and destroying property.*

In 1942, Franz George Eisenhut, who had founded the Merkur Leather Factory in Palanka, was assassinated by the Serbian Partisans. *He was the first victim in our town. He was the son of the*

*world-famous painter, Franz Eisenhut, whose masterpiece was
"Schlacht bei Zenta." The Eisenhuts were living in their house in Ilok.
The hills were ripe with grape fields when the Partisans came and
demanded that either he come out or they would kill his Viennese-born
wife and their two children. When he came out, he was captured, killed,
and cut to pieces. His body was brought back in a sheet to our village
for burial. After that incident, many people fled including Eisenhut's
mother.*

In the summer of 1943, heavy American bombers flew over
Palanka. No bombs fell, but young Kathe will never forget the eerie
blackness of that night sky. She and her family were gathered around
a small radio, which finally announced that the planes had passed
over the Carpathian Mountains en route to Russia with supplies.

By September of 1944, all that was open in Palanka was one cinema. It was apparent that the tide of war was running against the
Germans, and that the battlefield was now dangerously approaching
the regions inhabited by the Danube Swabians, which up to that
point had been spared the ravages of war. *We saw more and more
bombers flying over the Batschka to Russia. You could tell they were
carrying heavy loads of artillery from just the sound. Once, a bomb was
dropped on an island near the Danube. One plane crashed out of the
black sky onto a house that was owned by a sick woman with a young
daughter, but from what I remember, the house was empty at the time.*

Late fall of 1944 was the last draft. Many of the draftees had just
turned 17. With no military training, they were sent to fight in
Budapest, where most of them perished. One of the young soldiers
was Kathe's cousin Wilhelm Bautz, who was never able to send letters home to his widowed mother. Among his fallen comrades were
Franz Bautz, Niki Schon, and Hansi Griesbach. Kathe's father Anton
Karl also was drafted due to a clerical error on his birth certificate
making him 10 years younger. A town representative suggested he
report to the German *Hodschag* to fix the mistake, but Anton never
went because shortly thereafter, the Russian troops and Partisans
moved in.

The citizens had to make quick decisions: to flee or remain. Those who chose to leave did so by ship or by horse and wagon. The first refugees the Palankans saw were from the Banat. They were headed west, carrying whatever belongings they could on wagons. *They worried about how far they could get and whether the corn for the horses would last. In Palanka, those who joined the refugees had family in the German Army. The wagon trek left our town on October 11, traveling through Hodschag, Baja, Veszprem, and Vienna. In Nickolsberg, the horses and wagons had to be handed over to the armed forces.*

Two empty freighters on the Danube became the transport for some fleeing Palankans. *Our famous poet and veterinarian Johann Petri left with horses and returned home to Schowe, which is north of Novi Sad. He fled Yugoslavia in 1950 and died in Austria seven years later.*

Kathe relates her sister Elisabeth's story of hardship. Elisabeth had been very ill. Her husband was now in the German Army, and she and her young son Otto were among the last group of people fleeing the area. *She came to Palanka from Ilok with whatever she could carry, including a suitcase of kunas, Croatian currency. My family went with her and Otto to the Neu Palanka train station to say our goodbyes. We cried bitterly, not knowing if we would ever see each other again. After a few hours on the train, Elisabeth realized that she did not have any Hungarian money, but she could not return at that point to Palanka, since no trains were going south. The trip was bearable because the local town mayors made sure that shelters were made available in schools where the refugees were provided with food. The train moved on, north to Silesia and then south to Graz. It was here Elisabeth met her in-laws, who had left with two oxen and the horses, which were stolen by the Partisans. Elisabeth, Otto, and the Griesbachs were able to stay with Vicky-Tante, a widowed cousin from Novi Sad who had come to Graz. The elder Mr. Griesbach died that December. When a new transit camp opened near Leoben Austria, Elisabeth and Otto stayed there. I learned years later that they were at Camp Trofaiach. Food was rationed, but meals were prepared. Blankets were distributed. Schools for children were opened. The Lavundis received news from her via the Red Cross in February of 1945, and sent back the reply: "Parents are not home anymore. Parents and sisters are alive." My parents met her in Austria two years later.*

Others, like the Lavundi and Karl families, decided to stay in Palanka. Kathe explains this fateful decision: *We did not know what to do and where we could possibly go to. What would happen to us? Deep sorrows had disrupted our lives. One morning I met Prelate Grieser, who was the religion professor in Palanka. He told me that the Serbian officials from Alt Palanka had promised him and the Palankan people protection. We knew this was a promise that could not be kept. Terrible times were coming. Until now, we were not short of anything. We had enough food; we had shelter. Going to Germany was certainly not an option. We had never even been to Germany or Austria. We had no familial connections to the Fatherland. We knew that those countries were starving. The towns were bombed out and there were no shelters. We knew this to be true because a neighbor, Lady Eisenhut, had a daughter in Munich to whom she mailed food and soap and even a prepared pig. Why should we leave? Winter was coming. Here at home we had a full crop of wheat and sunflowers. We had pigs, horses, chickens, cows, geese. We hoped we might survive if we stayed in our homeland. After all, we had no enemies, we had no one in the army, we never had weapons.*

Early fall 1944. The death knell sounded for the Danube Swabians. Tito's Anti Fascist Council convened at Jajce in Bosnia and declared, without judicial process, that Danube Swabians were "enemies of the people and traitors," and thus disenfranchised. All property would be confiscated, and there would be systematic mass liquidations, deportation, and extermination. The fighters' reward would be the homes, farms, and livestock of those who had been exiled or murdered.

CHAPTER SEVEN

Bearing Witness:
October and November, 1944

Now you stand pale,
Condemned to wintry wandering,
Like smoke,
Which always seeks the colder climates.
The crows caw
And are city bound in whirring flight;
Soon it will snow
Woe to him who has no home

From *Isolated* by Frederich Nietzsche (1844-1900)

It was as if the clock had stopped ticking, as if time had come to a halt. By October of 1944, half the population had fled Palanka. Houses were empty. The Hungarian government had also left the Batschka. Kathe describes October and November of 1944 as the most horrible time for those who stayed behind. Beatings and killings happened daily.

Soon after the many refugees left their ancestral homeland, Red Army troops had marched in, followed by units of Tito's Partisan army. The German Army was still situated on higher ground in Sharengrad across the Danube until Easter of 1945. *They kept shelling Palanka with heavy artillery. The Russians and Partisans had nothing but hatred towards us. They were sadistic. They looted homes and raped women. Many of the women taken at gunpoint from their families were brought to Pancevo in Belgrade, where they were kept in cages and repeatedly raped by Tito's Partisan troops . Many became infected with syphilis, and to stop the disease from spreading, all of the women were taken to a remote meadow where they were shot to death.*

My godmother's eldest daughter, Theresia Engelbrecht, who had three young children, was raped by several Russian soldiers. When she discovered she was pregnant by one of her attackers, she lost her mind and eventually died in Schove Camp. Her children were shipped to Serbia. It was total anarchy. We stayed indoors and locked the windows and wooden shutters.

I remember one day when I saw troops from Novi Sad walking on the street. They passed our house dressed in many kinds of uniforms. At night they would look for shelter. This night, we heard a strong knock at the gate. Then, a colony of 50 or so men entered and occupied our home. They brought along two dead sheep to cook. They found our summer kitchen in the smokehouse, which had two pigs which we had slaughtered and smoked. One belonged to a neighbor, Mrs. Schimandy, a Hungarian woman who came to our house each morning for fresh milk. The soldiers brought the smoked pork into each room, chopping them up with hatchets on our finest tables, and left the sheep behind. They found wine and brandy in the basement, and barrels of wine were shot open, flooding the basement floor. My sister Maria Theresia and I were hidden in our secret room. It was in between two bedrooms and the door was covered by large furniture. The room was narrow and had one window and a twin bed. At times, my cousins Katharine, Kathe, and Resl Bautz hid in that room. This night it was very dark. We heard noise and were fearful one of us would sneeze, which would have proved fatal had we been discovered.

When the Hungarian government vacated the Batschka, they had handed the finances and city hall over to two men from Palanka. These men were assigned to meet the Partisans, the new government. *One was Wagner Wilmos, a wealthy, respected citizen and the other was Dr. Staudt, a Hungarian judge who was the son-in-law of Mrs. Schimandy. These men were ready to hand over everything, but instead they were taken to the registry of the fields called "Katasteramt." First, they were put into the high school. The judge's wife, Lonti, brought a blanket for him, but she was not able to find him. When she came back to our house for milk, she was hysterical, crying that she would never see her husband again. They had a one-year-old son with curly hair like an angel. She would later move to Hungary with her son to stay with her mother-in-law.* The Partisans grabbed Nikolaus Hepp, who had published a book on Palanka in 1930. They took him around the village on a wagon, demanding that he point out German men on the street. The men were picked up and taken to the "Katasteramt" near the park. Radios were turned on full blast so that the tortured screams could not be heard. They were never seen again.

At the end of October, 200 men were arrested and murdered in the Acacia Forest. On November 7th, 184 men were captured, imprisoned, and tortured. Some were taken to the coal mines in *Vrdnik Srem* (Serbia), where they were forced to do hard labor. *One of the men could barely walk and was thrown into a ditch and killed. Our neighbor, Franz Schon, who was a barrel maker and my father's godmother's son, was also killed. The people at home were deathly afraid for those first few weeks until a government was formed. But, if you had a personal enemy, you could be sure that harm would come to you. I had heard a story from my Grandfather Johann that in 1918, when the Batschka became Yugoslavia, Serbian and Gypsy civilians came into the house looking for money and other valuables. They began to beat him with a rifle until one man shouted "Stop!" That man was a Serbian horse dealer from whom my grandfather had bought many horses.*

Some of the prisoners who were taken to Vrdnik were thrown into the freezing waters, where Partisans randomly shot them. Prisoners were forced to march to Vrdnik barefoot and without winter clothing. *The fate of a rich Hungarian, Karl Cservenyi, and his brother was even worse. They had their eyes stabbed out and their noses and hands broken. Leopold Rohrbacher [in his book Ein Volk Ausgeloscht)] writes that they were skinned and had their genitals cut by women Partisans.*

In mid-November, the Partisans rounded up the remaining men and threw them into a concentration camp in Neusatz; among those was Rev. Professor Hans Grieser who managed to flee the camp in 1946. *Grieser is considered a national hero because he was the first wit-*

ness to tell the world, including Pope Pius XII at a private audience, about the horrible suffering and massacres of our people.

Before Christmas of 1944, 8,000 women between the ages of 18 and 35, and 4,000 men were shipped to Russia to work in the ancient cold coal mines.

Kathe was 16 years old and still has terrorizing recollections of her own family's torment and daily struggle to stay alive and together. Her maternal grandparents, Michael and Rozalia Pautz (nee Schoen) were living in New Palanka , a block from St. Elizabeth. *My grandfather was 74 at the time and had bad eyesight. He was still plowing the fields, because his youngest son had died from kidney disease. Grandfather was hoping that his grandson would one day take over running the farms. One morning, the Russian troops entered Grandfather's home and stole his watch that he had received at his confirmation. Then other Russian soldiers came and demanded watches. Because he could not produce any more, Grandfather was mercilessly beaten until his body was black and blue and he could not move. My mother was crying as she told me what she had witnessed.*

After their home also was being ransacked by Russian troops, Kathe's grandmother Rozalia Pautz's brother Johann Schoen and his wife Elisabeth were picked up and taken to the local property registry. *Their only crime was that their unmarried daughter Elisabeth was noted on the records but was not home because she was in hiding. Later that day, my mother opened the bedroom window to air out the room. Her aunt Elisabeth, Johann's wife, walked across the street from the park alongside the "Katasteramt." She briefly slowed down a few steps from the open window and quietly said, "I may not talk to anyone, I may not say what I heard. But your uncle Hans does not live anymore." And she kept walking to her home three blocks away and was never picked up.*

Everyone lived in fear for their lives, terrified of even being seen talking with their neighbors. *Finding out about the fate and whereabouts of friends and loved ones was nearly impossible, because of a fear of being deemed an enemy of the state. But, as was the case with Johann, once in a while precious information was relayed.*

Another neighbor was not so fortunate. The Reiss family were wealthy Hungarians who owned many fields called a *puszta*. *Mrs. Reiss hired a Slovak taxicab to drive her to Novi Sad. She paid a premium price for the short ride, and the driver demanded more money because he told her the road was bad and his tires were getting damaged. She refused. Not long after that incident, she was reported and picked up along with over 200 others who were also rounded up for being perceived as an enemy.*

One evening, the Partisans picked up a group of young boys 13 to 16 years old. *One of the boys was my cousin's son, Josef Karl, who was 15. They were tied together with a long rope and dragged to the Locust Woods. There they were ordered to shovel a grave. They were told to undress and climb into the shallow ditch, where they were shot. Josef had wanted to become a priest. His father, my cousin, witnessed the tying up of the young boys as he looked through an open roof tile.*

Because half of the population had fled and many had been killed, farms were not harvested, and everyone now was required to bring in the corn harvest. *A drummer would announce at each corner that we had to march a long distance to the fields. It was the fall, but it was very cold and very wet. I had a painful injury, probably a broken bone, on my left foot, and it was badly swollen. I was barely able to walk, and even though I tried to be brave, one night I came home crying because it hurt so much.*

Yet there were many selfless acts of kindness from friends. *Kathe continues her story. That night, around 6 PM, there was a loud knock on the door and a voice asking to be let in. I opened the door to find a man I knew. He was a beggar, an invalid who walked with a cane. He would come to our house every Wednesday, and we would never turn him away without giving him food. He never forgot that, for this night, he came in and sat on a chair. "Do not cry, my friend," he said to me in German, trying to comfort me, "I will watch over you and you will be safe."*

Kathe went to bed. She watched the curtains blowing gently in the night. She watched the stars shine down on the darkness, wondering if it might be the last night in the place of her birth.

CHAPTER EIGHT

From Homeland to Hell
1944-1946

There you stand, castle of my fathers,
Faithful and firm in my mind,
And you have disappeared from the earth,
The plow passes over you.
But I will arouse myself,
With my lyre held in my hand,
And roam the breadth of the earth
And sing from land

From *The Castle Boncourt* by Adalbert von Chamisso
(1781-1838)

Novembre 1944. People were forbidden to leave their village. *There were no busses or trains running. Since we lived close to the town center, we were the first family the Partisans came to for transport of their personnel. Dad put a black leather seat on the wagon. The soldiers taunted him. He was shown his stolen watch and told that he had to be in a certain place at a certain time or he would be killed. Sometimes he had to hit his horses to make them travel faster. In the late afternoon the following day, I looked out of our window. On the street towards the Locust Woods were about 20 to 30 people walking with shovels. They were not German townspeople. I became terrified. What is this? Oh God, are they going to kill us all?*

The forced expulsion of the remaining Batschka Donauschwaben was beginning, and Palankans would be the first to be exiled. The Protestant villages of the Batschka were very tight-knit and organized. Before the Communist onslaught, and along with their pastor, the residents fled their homes in Pasicevo, Schowe, Jarek, and

Tschervenka. The first two villages were turned into internment and work camps. The camp consisted of several hundred homes. Because the villages were not fenced in with barbed wire, there were Partisan and citizen guards stationed around the clock with instructions to kill anyone attempting to leave. In early 1945, two more liquidation camps would be set up in Gakova and Kruschiwl.

Religious leaders were no exception to the expulsion and work camps. *Our priests were sent to Novi Sad. Reverend Peter Weinert was in his seventies and had to cut wood all day. Reverend Johann Grieser was also there. Reverend Weinert died within a few months in Reverend Grieser's arms.* In 1988, Father Wendelin Gruber would write his personal story, *In the Claws of the Dragon: Ten Years Under Tito's Heel.*

Christmas, 1944. The holiest time of the year, which held such religious significance and precious memories, was especially horrific in the camp. Women between 18 and 35 years of age were shipped to Russia to work in the coal mines. *They were packed into cattle cars. It was freezing cold that year, and there was very little food. For the trip that took weeks, they lived in inhumane conditions and constantly feared for the future.*

Once the Partisans took control of Palanka, escape was impossible. *The Partisans had nothing but hate towards us and a desire for revenge. Because we spoke German, we were scapegoats for the behavior of the German Reich in Eastern Europe. Most of our men were arrested and thrown into the concentration camp at Neusatz. Women and children and old men were left behind, but now, armed Partisans went from house to house to take a census. All the people with German surnames would be interned. They asked for proof of our nationality. Those who were forced out were given less than 15 minutes to pack clothes and provisions; some of the victims who were not in favor were not even allowed to take anything with them. At about 1:00 in the afternoon on November 29th, two troops with rifles came to our home and called out our names, telling us to leave the house. There was no question that we were German by our name, Karl. Some people with Slavic names tried to declare their nationality as Slav, and that bought them some time, but eventually they too were picked up. My brother-in-law Emil Lavundi had been born and schooled in Gradisckka, Croatia. Because his mother was Croatian, he was registered as a Croat, and so he was safe for a while.*

Maria, Emil's wife, and their young son Wilhelm were allowed to remain. Kathe has painful images of that day, because her mother also was taken away by the Partisans. *My sister Maria Theresia fainted in the corridor. I walked out to the gate with my mother and asked her what I should do. "Go back to your sister, she needs you." And that's what I did. The guard did not see me go back to the house. Thank G-d. I lived with the Lavundis until February of 1946, but I feared every day about what would happen to us all. All of us experienced anxiety wondering when they would come and pick us up.*

The day her mother was taken away, Kathe's father was at work transporting Tito's soldiers and would not be home until later that night. When Anton Karl arrived back in Palanka, he knew that something was not quite right. *All of the doors were open; the animals were loose and wandering about. I told him what had happened earlier, that Palankans were being driven out, and that the Partisans, armed with rifles, barged into all of the houses and told the people to leave, to go outside. There were so many people there, from all over. The march of all the Palankan Germans began and that they had taken mother. Dad turned white as a sheet. He could not eat. He went to his bed in his house for the last time.*

To this day, and like many survivors, Kathe relives this terror and mental anguish in troubling recurrent dreams. *I go through the house. What shall I take? This? That? A coat? Some jewelry? I know they are waiting outside. I rush...I rush....*

Kathe later found out that the prisoners, all Palankan residents, were taken to the Jutte Factory at the end of town, where they stayed outside in the cold and freezing rain. Her mother, grandparents, and brother Josef's family were also there, as were her brother Tony's widow and daughter.

On November 30, 1944, Kathe saw her father cry for the first time. She watched him leave their house to go to *Stara* (Old) Palanka to report his whereabouts the previous day. *Dad paused for a moment at the front door, looked at the yard with Emil Lavundi's workshop in the back. Tears were running down his cheeks as he said, "It took so long to get all of this done, and now it is gone. It is all gone." He could not speak anymore and just hugged me tightly and kissed me goodbye.*

When Anton arrived in Stara, he was given a wagon to transport horses to the Partisans in the Jutte Factory. He saw all the people who were already there, including my mother. He took her and the others on the wagon and the 60 kilometer trek from Palanka to Pasicevo began. Those who were sick, elderly, or disabled were transported by wagon. Others were forced to march in the bitter cold weather with whatever possessions they had managed to take.

My mother and father were in Pasicevo until February of 1947. Pasicevo was surrounded by armed guards. The refugees were separated into two groups. Those who could work were sent to labor camps. Those who couldn't were transported to the camp in Jarek. *My mother's parents were sent to Jarek. Leaving her parents was devastating to my mother. My grandparents cried uncontrollably. My grandfather told my mother, "If and whenever you get out of this, you must leave this 'gesindel' (proletariat place) and go to America. Go. Go." He had a cousin who had left Palanka before World War I and was living in Trenton, New Jersey. My parents would never see their parents again.*

It was heartbreaking for the grandparents who were sent to Jarek, where many of them would die. My parents would stay in Pasicevo until 1947. My mother told me years later, "I heard the children crying 'I cannot go alone. You have to come with me.' Soldiers would beat the crying children running after their mothers with their with rifle butts."

Staying alive in Jarek from 1944-1946 was difficult. The prisoners were not allowed to cook. *A woman Partisan rode on her horse each day, and if she saw smoke coming out of the chimney, she would stop. The people would be beaten. But the prisoners would secretly prepare food by using two stones to grind corn into flour. The children were* so malnourished that their bellies were extended. The camp was infected with lice. The elders and children quickly perished. The dead skeletal bodies were picked up daily, thrown on the wagon, one on top of the other and dumped into unmarked graves. It was undignified. Oma, my grandma, died in August of 1945, and my Opa, grandpa, died two months later, both in an unmarked grave. There was no salt given to the prisoners, only one corn on the cob. A few were able to sustain themselves by eating grass. Elisabeth Lusch, the sister of Kathe's fraternal grandfather, existed on turnip leaves and dandelions. Some children crawled out during the night and went into the Hungarian village of Temerin, begging for food and then sneaking back into the camp again.

Outsiders were allowed, provided they had a permit, to bring packages of food and blankets to the camps. *In early January, 1945, with a permit obtained by Emil, my sister Maria Lavundi visited the camps at Pasicevo and Jarek. She was taken there by our horse and wagon driven by "Deda," the grandpa of Emil's apprentice boy, Radomir. The wagon was filled with packages of food and other necessities brought to our house by Hungarians who had family and friends in the camps. It was snowing hard and difficult to see, and they got lost a few times along the way. Once at Pasicevo, Maria was allowed to just leave the packages for the parents, which they did get. In Jarek, she had to see the Kommandant, who sent for her people to pick up the packages. She waited and waited. My grandfather Pautz Michael did not come, so she left the packages for him and my aunts. In a long letter from my grandpa, written in Gothic letters that was smuggled out of Jarek, we learned that the family did not receive all of what we sent. Grandpa also said that he was rushing so much to see his grandchild, but when he came around the corner, her wagon was already turning into another street. He never saw her again.*

In March, Kathe went with her brother-in-law, Emil, to visit her parents in the work camp. *It was Sunday, and those who remained in the village were home. People washed their clothes and hung them in the sun to dry. When we got to the camp, my dad was in bed. His body was filled with fluids and he could not see well. He was losing his eyesight. Mother was so skinny that her clothes just hung on her body. Each day my dad would come back to the camp from the mill where he worked with a little flour for my mother. Up until now, they were able to survive because my sister brought them food. But it was not enough, and when I left them that day, I was sure I would never see my parents again. Luckily, Emil was able to get my dad medication in Novi Sad, and so he was able to survive the camp.*

Still at home in Palanka, and with a full house, harvest, and farm animals, Emil was ordered to repair Russian trucks. Kathe and her sister took care of the animals at home. *We kept thinking that this would not be forever.*

During that summer of 1945, Kathe went to the market to purchase vegetables when someone called her name from across the street. *It was Mr. Bogschutz, Ritzl's father and the brother of my sister Elisabeth's mother-in-law, Maria Griesbach. He was marching with a group of camp prisoners. I called back to him in German, telling him that Elisabeth, Otto, and Maria's aunt were in Graz, that Heinrich Griesbach was a POW in Bosnia. After the prisoners passed by, a tall, dark Serb, a Petric city employee, stood in front of me and asked me who I was and where I lived. I told him. He said, "Still today you will follow them." I was very scared and ran home and told my sister and brother-in-law what happened. I expected to be picked up and sent to a camp.*

As 1945 was coming to an end, government elections were held in private homes. The people assumed that the vote was to select either King Peter II or Marshall Tito. *This was just propaganda,* Kathe says. After the overwhelming electoral victory, Tito was confirmed as the prime minister and the minister of foreign affairs of the DFY. The country was soon renamed the *Federal People's Republic of Yugoslavia* (FPRY) and later renamed the Socialist Federal Republic of Yugoslavia (SFRY). On November 29, 1945, King Peter II was formally deposed by the Yugoslav Constituent Assembly. One of the houses where the mock elections were held was that of Anton Karl and Emil Lavundi. *We had to empty two rooms to house their machines and materials. Once all the people came to our home to vote, they saw what we had in the house. The garden was in full bloom with football chrysanthemums in all colors. We had a beautiful veranda and cement tiles. Emil's workshop for his successful and expanding knitting machine business was equipped with all sorts of machinery. That was an incentive for the Partisans to intern the remaining members of the Lavundi and Karl families and take over the house, land, and business.*

On a bitter cold February morning in 1946, three Partisans with rifles arrived at the only home Kathe had known since childhood. *The soldiers called out the names of those to be interned: "Emil Lavundi. Maria Lavundi. Wilhelm Lavundi. Katharina Karl. You are to leave the house immediately and will be interned." All four of us were standing in front of Emil's workshop. Emil said, "We are not leaving this house. Never. You will have to shoot us dead." The Partisans threatened to tie us up and pull us to the camp, so Emil gave in. We walked two blocks to the Ovoda, a school on Farmer's Street. There we were searched. All gold jewelry and money was taken from us and thrown into the corner of the room. We were given a place in the city hall building called the "Gemeindhaus." My room was near the front entrance. Luckily, I had grabbed my good navy crombi-velvet winter coat with fur trim. It kept me warm, and I rolled it up as a pillow under my head when sleeping. It was never stolen from me. I was lucky.*

In February of 1946, Kathe was sent to the Palanka camp, where she and the others were stripped of all their valuables. Though not as bad as Jarek, conditions were inhumane and food was scarce. *We slept on straw on the floor. There was a kitchen where they cooked whatever little food was provided to us. We would have flour soup at 6:00 in the morning, and then report for our work assignments at 7:00 AM. Some would be told to work in the fields. Those who could not walk the long distance would be pulled out of the crowd, beaten with rifles, and left to die. For dinner, we had bean soup. Corn was used to make bread. Some of the prisoners were sold to outsiders for day work, which was paid for, and the money was given to the commandant. We liked to go outside of the camp because at least we were fed. My sister worked for a baker for several months. She and her nine-year-old son Willi slept there.*

Kathe had several jobs while in Palanka Camp. *I was sold as a maid to an innkeeper on the outside of the camp. For a while I stayed in a house occupied by the camp Kommandant, watching his sick one-year-old son. I was then sold to a rich Slovak family in Glozan for three months. I was picked up at the camp by the pastor of town, who drove me to my job in a horse-drawn wagon. I was treated fairly well. I knitted sweaters. My bed was in the kitchen and was used in the daytime by the family's son who suffered from Hepatitis. From there, I was returned to the camp and sent with a group to Plavna for fieldwork alongside the Danube. I could see Vukover on the other side of the river. I knew then I would somehow escape.*

CHAPTER NINE

Flight to Freedom

America, you've got it better
Than our old continent. Exult!
You have no decaying castles
And no basalt.
Your heart is not troubled,
In lively pursuits,
By useless old remembrance
And empty disputes.
So use the present day with luck!
And when your child a poem writes,
Protect him, with his skill and pluck,
From tales of bandits, ghosts and knights.

To America by Johann Wolfgang von Goethe (1749-1832)

By the end of the summer of 1946, Kathe managed to escape to Vukovar by ferry, where she would attempt to flee to Osijek, Slavonia, where the Lavundi family was. *I met an old man who showed me a different route so that I would not be killed by guard dogs. He never asked me any questions, but he was surely my guardian angel. I was so scared because I did not have any ID.*

In January, 1947, a Croatian man risked his life when he took me to his sister's family in Baranja, where I would be able to hide until there was opportunity to escape Yugoslovia to Hungary, and then to Austria were my parents and sister were. She became almost like a sister to me and we still keep in touch.

Between late 1946 and 1947, sentry security became even more lax in the camps, and many Palankan prisoners were able to escape from the camps and flee Yugoslavia from over the border. There were several social and political conditions that contributed to the prisoner population and lessened vigilance at Gakowa, and economic incentives that prompted people to assist the fleeing prisoners.

Johann Grieser had been Kathe's religion professor when she was in school. Interned in 1944, he escaped from Novi Sad to Hungary in 1946. From there he went to Austria, and eventually to Italy. Having documented the treatment of the ethnic Germans, he went to the Vatican in Rome for an audience with Pope Pius XII and the World Press. The Pope could only ensure that the people would be released from the camps.

So it happened that indeed the prisoners in the South Batschka camps were relocated to Gakova and Krusiwl, both in close proximity to the Hungarian border. By that time, over 38,000 ethnic Germans had perished from malnutrition, syphilis, starvation, malaria, cold, and hunger.

There were two means of transport headed from Gakovo to Hungary. One was called the White Transport, where money was paid by the prisoners to the Partisans to march them in knee-high snow to the border. Kathe's parents were among that group of fleeing refugees. The second mode were the so-called Black Transports, which often times did not succeed because they were run by civilians.

In September 1947, Kathe had a plan to escape from Yugoslavia and join her family in Austria. From the vantage point of the hills where Kathe was in hiding, she could see Bezden in the Batschka. *Gakova was not fenced in with wire, and the camp was guarded by sentries. Even though the punishment if found was death, it was possible to sneak past the guards and go begging or attempt to escape. I could see the kids from Gakova who went begging, sneaking in and out of Gakova. I made a decision to leave.*

It was a sad moment when I told my dear friends who were now like family to me that I had to go and find my parents in Austria. After leaving her friends, Kathe stopped in Osijek to say yet another difficult goodbye to her sister Maria and nephew Willi. *She would have loved to come with me, but Emil was interned in Pozarecac with war crimi-*

nals, and she could not leave him. While Emil was still in Pozarecac, Maria and her son were picked up in Osijek and sent to Rudolfsgrad/Knicanin Camp. It would be 10 years until the Lavundi family would arrive in the USA.

Kathe went to Bezden. *In Bezden, I sneaked into Gakova with the beggar kids, hoping to get the chance to cross the border. I was not registered and I had no food. I was able to stay hidden in the attic. I had a small amount of money that my sister Maria had given me to get to Hungary. Only Black Transports were possible. I paid 600 dinar to a landsmann, the father of two girls I knew. He paid a woman named Leni who ran a Black Transport. But we were caught at the Hungarian border and we were all taken back to Gakova, where we were punished by being kept in a basement for three days without food. Leni was not there, and I never got back my money, because she returned it to the Landsmann who had given it to her.*

Kathe now had no money and no rations. Though she was very weak, she was still determined to escape Yugoslavia. *I found two young men who had a lot of stuff to carry in two suitcases. They did not have any money, but as leaders they had accumulated things that they hoped to sell. They let me pay my way by carrying their luggage. We met at a house at midnight, and when the sentry guards changed shifts, we snuck out of Gakova. I was sick, hungry, and thirsty. My knees were shaking I was so weak. The suitcases were very heavy.* This time, however, Kathe made it across the border to Hungary. For several days, she and the young men worked on a farm. *As payment, the farmer took us by horse to Mohacs* [a town in the Baranja on the right bank of the Danube] *where we bought train tickets to St. Gotthard in Austria, where we would find someone to take us to the English zone.*

There were frightening moments along the way. They arrived at their destination, but the man they found to take them left them in the Russian zone. *At the Russian zone in Burgenland, we were stopped. Two Russian soldiers wanted to take us to the Commandant, who would have returned us back to Yugoslavia. When the Russian soldiers began arguing about the luggage, we saw our chance and ran off, empty-hand-*

ed, into the woods. We saw a man plowing across a narrow river and yelled to him. We yelled to him,"What zone is this?" "English," he replied. "Just go a little more and you will find the custom station." So we walked until we met the custom officer, who greeted us with, "Welcome to Austria! You are not far from Furstenfeld in Styria, a transit camp." We found our way there. Many refugees came to that camp, which was filled with barracks. Dates, names, and places were written on the walls in hopes of finding lost family members. My mother came to pick me up in the transit camp because I was still a minor.

In October of 1947, after an arduous journey and crossing many borders, Kathe arrived in Austria and was reunited with her parents, sister, and nephew from whom she was separated for three years. *Austria was so beautiful. We were very welcomed there. We lived in barracks for eight years until we were able to emigrate to America. It was where the military and POWs had been housed. We literally had nothing. Food was scarce, but the Austrians generously shared their food tickets with us and treated us like the other citizens. We were very poor, but we were free! We worked hard to save money for tickets on the passenger ship that would take us to America, but most of what we earned went to food. I went to an English school to learn the English language and bookkeeping. I was fortunate to get a good paying job in the office of the Royal Army Ordinance Corps for the English troops stationed in Austria.*

In 1956, during her last days in Austria, Kathe met Nikolaus Marx, the man whom she would marry. Born in Palanka in 1928, Nikolaus was now a metal worker living in Germany. He was visiting family in Villach, and when he heard the name Karl mentioned by a mutual friend, he remembered having a classmate with that name in elementary school back in Palanka. *He came for a visit and there was a connection, a bond between us, from the old country. There was a trust because of our backgrounds. We saw each other for the next three days until my family had to leave Villach for Le Havre, Paris, from where we would then travel to Germany to visit my mother's brother and his family. On April 6, we boarded the SS America. We arrived in New York Harbor on April 11, 1956, sailing by the beautiful Statue of Liberty which welcomed us to our new home and a life of freedom.*

Kathe and her parents moved in with her sister Elisabeth and her family, who already were living in Philadelphia. Anton found work as a landscaper, and Kathe was hired as a bookkeeper. *It had been 13 years since our property was confiscated in Palanka. I thought this was the nicest house in the world and that we were the most blessed people in the world because we were all together again.* Meanwhile, Kathe and Nikolaus continued to correspond, and in January 1957, Nik emigrated to the United States. He and Katharina Karl were married on May 4, 1957 in a ceremony attended by family.

In 1957, the Lavundi family also arrived in America, also settling in Philadelphia, not far from the Griesbachs. *Dad passed away less than one year after being in America and he never saw us become proud citizens of our new homeland where we worked hard to be successful, just as we had done in the old country.*

CHAPTER TEN

Roots

There in distant Hungary,
 a friendly hamlet small and bright
is cuddled in a woody site,
content in mild prosperity.
So tranquil on the village edge,
a little cottage holds its pledge,
within its warming walls to guard
 my world and all that stirs the heart.

Nikolaus Lenau

It has been over six decades since young Katherina Karl apprehensively stepped off the USS America in New York City. Like her kinsmen who migrated from the Schwaben section of Germany to the Danube River region during the nineteenth and twentieth centuries, Kathe has assimilated into her adopted homeland. She is proud to be an American, but in the Swabian immigrant tradition, she remains staunchly committed to cherishing her ancestral heritage and passing down those traditions and history to her own children and grandchildren. She and her husband Nikolaus instilled, by example, a strong faith and work ethic in their daughter, Christine.

Nik, to whom Kathe was married for 45 years, passed away in September, 2002. *We had a good life together; he was a wonderful husband and dad. He worked hard all of his life so we could have a nice life and so that our daughter could go to college.* Their daughter, Dr. Christine Marx Telford, was raised to speak both English and German. She received her undergraduate degree in German literature, and went on to receive an MD from Duke University, where she now works as a medical researcher. In 1988, she married George

Telford III. They have two daughters. Rebecca Hope is a student at Oberlin College and Conservatory studying music. She is an accomplished violinist. Emily Faith attends Swarthmore College and is also a violinist.

In addition to being blessed with her own family, Kathe has an extended *Donauschwaben* family. She is one of the oldest members and a past officer of the Danube Swabian Association of Philadelphia and Vicinity, formed in 1957 by ethnic-German immigrants, and one of many such groups that make up the National Association of *Donauschwaben*. Evolving from the Danube Swabian Aid society in the 1950s established by new immigrants who arrived from Hungary, Romania, and the former Yugoslavia, the society strived not only to bring new immigrants together but to work with existing organizations such as the United German Hungarians, the Banater Club, and the Gewerbe Singing Society. The association formed a children's group, Ladies' Auxiliary, and soccer division. In 1962, the German Weekend Language School opened its doors.

As secretary to the Philadelphia Donauschwaben and an active member of the Ladies' Auxiliary, Kathe is involved all year long in organizing fundraising events and traditional festive and religious holidays, such as *Tag der Donauschwaben,* Danube Swabian Day, marked by joyous music and dances. *Kirchweih* dates back to the Middle Ages as a religious commemoration of the consecration of the Christian church. The annual much-awaited *Schlachtfest*, rendering of a pig, is a replication of the customary Danube Swabian village pig slaughter. In the old country, the butcher and food preparer was a local renowned farmer, and people came from the surrounding area to feast on wursts, salami, and ham. One of the more somber events is *Wallfahrt*, the pilgrimage. Every June, New York and Trenton Donauschwaben join their Philadelphia brethren in a symbolic walk to the St. John Neumann Shrine. This pilgrimage touches the heart of every Donauschwaben, as it remembers family and friends who were forced to leave their homeland when the Communist tide swept through Europe in the years 1944 through

1948. The memorial mass at the church is in honor of the people who died in the camps of Yugoslavia, Russia, and Baragan, Rumania, and for those who were forced out of their homes in East Prussia, Silesia, Hungary, Sudetenland, Bohemia, and Gotschee. The service is followed by a summer evening celebration of traditional Donauschwaben culture.

I have had the honor and humbling experience of meeting so many remarkable Holocaust survivors over the course of some 15 years. The majority admit that once they left their homeland after witnessing ruthless massacres and seeing or experiencing other unimaginable atrocities, they chose to bury their painful memories. Many survivors, not wanting to burden their children with terrifying stories of survival and near death experiences, would remain silent—rarely talking about their past. Others would talk frequently about what they had endured, about how fortunate their children were to be living in a free country where government-sponsored acts of genocide would not be possible. More disturbing, survivors sometimes say that few people wanted to hear what they had to say, even when they finally were prepared to break their silence. Children of survivors often talk about how their parents' relationships with them clearly were affected by what they had to endure during their concentration camp captivity. For a good many survivors, it is only when their grown children and grandchildren reopen the questions that the survivors give a voice to their unfathomable experiences.

It is a difficult journey for survivors of any genocide to return to their homeland, to relive the agony and the helplessness and rage, the pain and misery that are buried deeply like lava in a supposedly extinct volcano. But in 2009, Kathe, Christine, George, 16-year-old Rebecca, and 15-year-old Emily sojourned to Palanka, the land of their ancestors and place of Kathe's birth. *I think that not one week passed in my life that I did not remember Palanka. The memories of my childhood were alive in my memory, and I could picture my home, the churches, the schools, and the parks. Times with my family and friends remained in my heart always.* Of course, the Danube , once a vital source of life, once a river of doom and the victim's last gathering place, flows through all of those memories.

Rebecca Telford Marx, about the same age as her grandmother was during the Communist deluge, recorded her insightful and vivid impressions of Palanka: *It was a mix of old and new; glossy storefronts bordered pre-war homes and buildings were in varying stages of upkeep. My grandmother would tell me who used to live where, what they did for a living, and who their children were. What she remembered was incredible. In town, I imagined my relatives going to school and church, coming home after school, walking to the post office, sleeping over at a cousin's house. It was magnificent, and yet the beauty...was tempered by the solemnity of wartime tragedies that had occurred in and around the province. A solemn drizzle accompanied our group as we stood beneath the monument erected by the Donauschwaben. We walked along the Danube and [I] imagined dozens of young people who enjoyed the view we did every Sunday after church as we walked in the gracious shadows of the broad leafy trees.*

After sightseeing in Vienna, the Karl-Marx family travelled to Budapest, and then to Serbia to be able finally to mourn at the Black Cross Monument honoring the over 8,000 who starved and died in the Gakova Camp from 1944-1948. A place, too, to imagine the anguished cries of victims of crimes that were so outrageous that one wonders if there is any solace in mourning. Continuing south, Kathe drove past villages where there were once well cared for houses filled with love and laughing children. The years of neglect and destruction had taken a heavy toll. The landscape was ruined; a fitting lament, perhaps, for the snuffed-out lives never to return again.

Passing through the fields, Kathe's memories release echoes of long ago. *To my astonishment, the fields were seeded and green. It bloomed almost as if the fields were cared for by the Donauschwaben who once lived here. There was bountiful wheat and corn. Once again I saw the tall yellow sunflowers I so vividly remembered from my childhood. But yet a terrible sadness came over me. The good earth was still producing—almost as if nothing had ever happened.*

Entering through Obrovac in the Batschka Palanka municipality, Kathe and her family arrived in Palanka. *The first thing I noticed was the absence of the hemp factories and ponds. We approached the site of the Lavundi and Karl house. Our home was still there. The church was not visible because the Linden trees had grown so tall. As a child, I could see the time on the church clock tower from our home. The park alongside the church is still there, but gone are the big locust trees that shaded us from the afternoon sun.*

The following day, June 1, 2009, Kathe and her family attended 8:00 mass at St. Anthony's Church, which was Prelate Grieser's church. After the service, and with mixed emotions, Kathe returned to her *vaters-house* at 476 Cara Dusane. A friend had told the current owners, Dragica Milinkovic and her father, that Kathe would be arriving.

Kathe carefully recorded her immediate reactions: *Finally after 65 years, my longtime wish was fulfilled as I stood once again in front of my childhood home where I had felt so loved and safe. It is early morning and quiet. It all looks familiar, and at the same time unfamiliar. The entrance gate is different. It is lower. It used to be high so that Dad could pass through it when he returned from the fields driving a large horse-drawn wagon loaded with straw or hay. I opened the gate and the memories flooded back to that November when my parents would leave the house forever and I would not be reunited with them until 1947. I followed my mother to this gate when the soldiers came and read the list of the names to be interned, giving them just five minutes to leave. "Go back Katharina—your sister needs you." I saw my father the next day as he left the house to report to the authorities. He hugged me so hard, and I felt the tears rolling down his cheeks as he whispered, "It took so long to build all this and now we must go." I didn't want to let go. From now on, we were nobody, no identity, not free, just homeless. Our good and happy life and our childhood and youth, which was well guarded, was lost forever. From now on, there would be hardship, hunger, danger, and hard work. But what Tito's regime could not take from us was our faith that had been nurtured by our family, the* clergy in our religion classes, and the sisters in the Convent School. That is what helped all of us to survive those years.

Kathe feels the fluttering of her heart as the front door to her past opens. *Dragica and her dad greet us and invite us in for coffee and juice. As is the tradition, I have brought two gifts of coffee. The open veranda leading into the flower garden was still beautiful. I closed my eyes. I could see my family coming and going, the dogs, the stables, the animals in the barns, and Emil's workshop.*

Kathe shows her family the secret room where she and her sisters and cousins hid. She stands in the place in the hallway where Emil faced the soldiers and said, "Shoot us here and now. We are not leaving." *Then Dragica shows us her apartment, which is where Maria Theresia lived with her husband and young son, Willi. It's the room where my nephew was born. The same double doors with glass remained. We walked through the house and garden one last time. When we left, I turned back once for a final look at my childhood home, and then I kept walking.*

A last-minute decision was a visit to Kathe's maternal grandparents' house. *Niki Franz, a friend of mine and the new owner, came with us. We were not expected, and when the owner stepped out, he was somewhat skeptical. After telling him about my family and that I often slept at this house, I handed him a gift of coffee. He asked me why it took so long to come back! He invited us into his house and offered us schnapps. I looked at the backyard, which no longer had barns and stables. What was still there was a plaque with the name Willi Pautz. It was made by my grandfather for his grandson Willi who was supposed to take over the house, but who died in Budapest at a young age.*

The final and fitting stage of the pilgrimage was to the Danube, where the sparkling blue waters that for centuries was the lifeblood of the Danube Swabians once flowed red with their blood. *So many Sundays we strolled with our friends under the leafy chestnut trees to the banks of the Danube. I could still recall the Serbian girls bedecked in their finery. Because she knew that some of the happiest times of my youth were spent sledding and skating on the frozen waters, Christine suggested we take the same path together this day. I stared silently at the rows of tall trees pointed upward towards the skies. I looked across the calm and beautiful river to the town of Ilok, where Elisabeth and her family had lived until the catastrophe. There was a gray mist over the landscape as I listened to the serene lapping of the water and said farewell to my beloved homeland of Palanka.*

I was at peace. I had no resentment for those living in homes taken from my family and friends. Though it was more painful to handle than I thought, it was the right thing to do. After 65 years, I returned to my homeland to pay respect to the two million Donauschwaben killed out of revenge for crimes they never committed. I was aware that my grand-children wanted to know everything that happened to us and how much they needed a record to pass on to their children. Yes, it was right to come home again, to remember and pass on the tragic story of our peo-ple.

I think back to when I began this book, to Kathe's garden in Philadelphia. It strikes me that, like the seedlings she first nurtures in protective containers, Kathe's story—and those thousands of others—is one that began in the seemingly safe and idyllic storybook world of the Batschka Palanka . How unnatural that such a pastoral scene now hides deep beneath its soil, the remnants of such unspeakable violence and death, the victims in their final resting places in the cold water of the Danube, or beneath the earth, thrown into mass graves now covered with fields of green. Uprooted and exiled from their native land, the tenacious survivors eventually replanted them-selves on new soil. They readily would adapt and contribute to their new countries, but they neither would forget the land they first cul-tivated, nor the roots they carried with them. Those roots would become the flowers of all the tomorrows, and the seeds of hope for today.

Afterword

The subtitle of this book is *The Ethnic German Genocide in History and Memory*. Indeed, history and collective memory intersect, and together, contribute to our larger human understanding of events. Using public and private documents, historians linearly chronicle events and interpret the past as they perceive them. If we are to concur with Walter Benjamin's assertion, as noted in the Preface, that history is indeed written by the victors, we must also give credence to the subjectivity of history and that it deliberately can be manipulated for political ends. All history, one might argue, is memory as perceived by the author or as interpretation of the past. The past is not simply a list of events. Historical records are the means by which historians develop their interpretations of those events. Because interpretations differ, there is no single historical record, but various narrations of events each told from a different perspective.

Likewise, memory is only valid for the person who experiences the event and is always a synthesis of facts. In teaching about genocide, it is not enough to teach about facts and figures or about the historical context of recent or age-old ethnic, religious, or national conflict, as important as that may be.

Collective oral history, the abundant testimony of those who bore witness to modern crimes against humanity, gives history a voice, and becomes an essential historical source that both personalizes and validates the narrative. There are those who claim that survivor memory is too over laden with pathos, and therefore should be rendered unreliable. I strongly disagree. Genocides are atrocities inflicted by people on people. It is crucial that the human experience of the victims be told in the first person so that it may be at least partly understood.

Elie Wiesel, author of the iconic testimony *Night*, has argued of Auschwitz that only those who lived it in their flesh and in their minds can possibly transform their experience into knowledge. Others, despite their best intentions, can never do so. Essentially for Wiesel, if you have not lived it, you simply cannot represent it.

And so we listen. Though excruciatingly painful, we hear testimonies about events of extreme human and ethical significance to learn about and from the past. But knowledge is not a value that stands alone; knowledge must be connected to meaning and action and striving to improve ourselves.

And so we remember. We remember because we cannot forget and because memory is at the core of what makes us human— even when it comes to perhaps the most horrific, degrading events in modern history. We remember because we must never forget the inhumanity of which humans are capable. And we remember these despicable acts and intense suffering and cruelty because despite many who have and continue to stand against tyranny, hatred, and intolerance, genocides continue to occur. We remember too, to fortify ourselves against the kind of callous indifference that allows mass murderers to proceed unimpeded with their grisly deeds. While the indescribable world of death camps and mobile killing battalions cannot be redeemed, remembering is as close as we can come in the face of the ultimate inhumane event.

It is my hope that the tragic saga of the Danube Swabians will be added as a chapter in the annals of human atrocities. This dark spot in modern Western history must be recognized as a part of German history, European history, and the history of holocausts and genocides. It is only through awareness and understanding of the uniqueness of each, and the parallels between them, that we can foster a culture of tolerance and compassion for all the innocent souls who are victims of man's inhumanity to man, whatever their race, religion, or national origin. It's an assertion of our humanity, and it is our human obligation to pass on the torch of memory to future generations. It is not enough to curse the darkness of the past; we must illuminate the future.

END NOTES

Chapter One

1. Gaeta; Jones; See Terms and Conditions of the UN Genocide Convention and Resolution @ un.org/en/preventgenocide/docu-ment.shtml.
2. Totten Vol II, Jones.
3. Kiernan; Totten.
4. Works of Kuper.
5. Nussan Porter; Blox; Wallman et al.
6. Nussan Porter; Vardy and Hunt; Andreopoulos.
7. Bloxham and Moses; Works of Yehuda Bauer.
8. Nussan Porter; Andreopoulas.
9. Totten Vol. II; Jones.
10. Walliman et al.
11. Totten Vol. II; Bloxham and Moses.
12. Fein.
13. Fein.
14. Andreopoulos; Bloxham and Moses.
15. Totten Vol. II; Jones.
16. Andreopoulos.
17. Kiernan.
18. Durant.
19. Stanton.
20. Writings of Yehuda Bauer.

Chapter Two

1. Fuhrmann and Reuter.
2. Crankshaw.
3. Robinson; Singleton; Bell-Fialkoff.
4. Boatswright et al.; Writings of Bell-Fialkoff.
5. Boatswright et al.; Writings of Bell-Fialkoff.
6. Mocsy; Mehrdad Kia.
7. Thompson; Szuchman.

8. Thompson; Szuchman; Writings of Bell-Fialkoff.
9. Thompson; Szuchman.
10. Crankshaw; Mehrdad Kia.
11. Crankshaw; Mehrdad Kia.
12. Compiled from writings of Schindler, Kopp, and F. Schmidt.
13. Compiled from writings of Schindler, Kopp, and F. Schmidt.
14. Compiled from writings of Schindler, Kopp, and F. Schmidt.
15. Compiled from writings of Schindler, Kopp, and F. Schmidt.
16. Cox; Bideleux; Kann; Mocsy; Burleigh.
17. Cox; Bideleux; Kann; Mocsy
18. Cox; Bideleux; Kann; Burleigh.
19. Cox; Bideleux; Kann; Mocsy.
20. Compiled from writings of Schindler, Kopp, and F. Schmidt.
21. Compiled from writings of Schindler, Kopp, and F. Schmidt.
22. Compiled from writings of Schindler, Kopp, and F. Schmidt.
23. Schmidt. *Introduction*

Chapter Four
1. Tudela.
2. Silverman; Singleton.
3. Elazar; Lituchi.
4. O'Brien; Crankshaw.
5. Schram qtd. in Jakob Schmidt.
6. Silverman; Elazar.
7. Kann; Singleton.
8. Gilbert; Shepherd.
9. De Zayas *A Terrible Revenge*.
10. Elazar; Gilbert.
11. Elazar; Jasenovich.
12. Stavrianas; Kaplan.
13-14, Wachtel, Kaplan.
15-17. Gilbert; Cox.
18-19. Kaplan,Wachtel; Interview with Katharina Marx.
20. Cox; Kaplan.

Chapter Five

1. Refer to Chapters Two and Three for the larger framework of Palankan history; For Palanka history specifically, Jakob Schmidt and interview with Katharina Marx.

2 and 3. Quoted in Jakob Schmidt.

Teaching Guide

1. List of genocides compiled from the varied research of Kiernan, Szuchman, Jones, and Kuper.

Works Consulted and Cited

Andreopoulos, George, ed. Genocide: *Conceptual and Historical Dimensions* PA: University Pennsylvania Press, 1997.

Appelbaum, Stanley, ed. *Beruhmte Gedichte der Deutschen Romantik: Great German Poems of the Romantic Era.* NY: Dover Pub., 1995.

Banac, Ivo. *With Stalin Against Tito: Cominformist Splits in Yugoslav Communism.* NY: Cornell Univ. Pr., 1988.

Bauer, Dennis J. *A collection of Genealogical information of Palankaer-Americans and Related Family Members—1895 to 2008* (includes a history of the Donauschwaben in Palanka, Batschka, Austria-Hungary and the Trenton, NJ area). DVHH publication.

Bauer, Yehuda. *Holocaust and Genocide Studies. Vol 8: No.3* Oxford University Press, 2006.

_____. *History of the Holocaust.* NY: Scholastic Publishing 2001.

Bell-Fialkoff, Andrew. *The Role of Migration in the History of the Eurasian Steppe: Sedintary Civilization vs. Barbarian and Nomad.* NY: Palgrave MacMillan, 2000.

Benjamin of Tudela. *Itinerary of Benjamin of Tudela: Travels in the Middle Ages.* MT: Kessinger Publishers, 2004.

Bideleux, Robert and Ian Jeffries. *A History of Eastern Europe: Crisis and Change.* London: Routledge, 1998.

Bloxham, P. and A. Dirk Moses. *The Oxford Handbook of Genocide Studies.* UK: Oxford University Press, 2010.

Boatwright, Mary and D. Gargola and R. Talbert. *Brief History of the Romans.*, Ed. I. ed. UK: Oxford University Press, 2005.

Braham, Randolph, ed. *The Nazi's Last Victims: The Holocaust in Hungary*. MI: Wayne University Press, 2002.

Burleigh, Michael. *The Third Reich: A New History*. NY: Hill and Wang, 2001.

Carmichael, Cathie. *Ethnic Cleansing in the Balkans: Nationalism and the Destruction of Tradition*. UK: Taylor and Francis, Ltd.

Cornelius, Deborah. *Hungary in World War II: Caught in the Cauldron*. NY: Fordham University Press, 2000.

Courtois, Stéphane et al. *The Black Book of Communism: Crimes, Terror, Repression*. Cambridge: Harvard Univ. Press, 1999.

Cox, John K. *History of Serbia*. CT: Greenwood, 2002.

Crankshaw, Edward. *Fall of the House of Habsburg*. NY: Penguin, 1983.

De Zayas, Alfred Maurice. *The German Expellees: Victims in War and Peace*. New York: St. Martin's Press, 1993.

_____. *A Terrible Revenge: The "Ethnic Cleansing" of the East Germans, 1944-1950*. New York: St. Martin's Press, 1994.

Durant, Will. *The Story of Civilization.Volume I: Our Oriental Heritage*. NY: Simon and Schuster, 1976.

Elazar, Daniel. *Balkan Jewish Communities*. MD: University Press of America, 1987. Series: Jerusalem Center for Public Affairs for Jewish Community Studies.

Engelmann, Nikolaus. *The Banat Germans* Translated by John Michels. Bismarck, ND: University of Maryland Press, 1987.

Evans, Richard J. *In Hitler's Shadow: West German Historians and the Attempt to Escape from the Nazi Past*. NY: Knopf Doubleday Publishing Group, 1989.

Fein, Helen. *Genocide Watch*. CT: Yale University Press, 2008.

Feldtanzer, Oskar. *Short History of the Colonization of the Batschka Region with Special Attention to the German Immigration*. Translated by Doris Feldtanzer and Transliterated by Myrtle Feldtanzer.

Frey, Katherine Stenger. The *Danube Swabians: A People with Portable Roots*. Belleville, Ont., Canada: Mika Publishing Co., 1982.

Fulbrook, Mary. *The Divided Nation: A History of Germany 1918-1990* London: Oxford University Press, 1992.

Gaeta, Paola, ed. *UN Genocide Convention: A Commentary*. USA: Oxford University Press, 2009.

Fuhrmann, Horst, and Reuter. Germany in the High Middle Ages c. 1050-1200. [Campbridge Medieval Textbook] UK: Cambridge University Press, 1996.

Gilbert, Martin. Holocaust: *History of the Jews of Europe During the Second World War*. Henry Holt and Co., 1986.

Gilbert, Martin. *The Righteous: Unsung Heroes of the Holocaust*. Henry Holt and Co., 2004.

Gibbons, Edward. *The Decline and Fall of the Roman Empire. Vols. I,II,III*. Hugh Trevor-Roper, ed. NY: Knopf Doubleday, 1996.

Glenny, Misha. *The Fall of Yugoslavia*. NY: Penguin Publishers, 2007.

Gruber, Fr. Wendelin. *In the Claws of the Red Dragon: Ten Years Under Tito's Heel*. Toronto: St. Michaelswerk, 1988. Translated from German by Frank Schmidt.

Gruesome Harvest: The Allies' Postwar War Against the German People. CA: Institute for Historical Review, 1992.

Hewitt, Waterman, ed. *Poems of Uhland. German Edition*. SC: Bibliobazaar, 2009.

Jones, Adam. *Genocide*. CT: Taylor and Francis, 2006.

Kaltenegger, Roland. *Titos Kriegsgefangene: Folterlager, Hungermärsche und Schauprozesse* Graz : Leopold Stocker Verlag, 2001.

Kann, Robert. *A History of the Habsburg Empire 1526-1918*. CA: University of CA Press, 1974.

Kaplan, Robert. *Balkan Ghosts: A Journey Through History*. NY: Picador, 2005.

Kierrnan, Ben. *Blood and Soil: A World History of Genocide and Extermination from Sparta to Darfur*. CT: Yale University Press, 2009.

Koehler, Eve Eckert. *Seven Susannahs: Daughters of the Danube*.

Milwaukee: Danube Swabian Societies of the US and Canada, 1976.

Komjathy, Anthony and Rebecca Stockwell. *German Minorities and the Third Reich*. London: Holmes and Meier Publishers, Inc., 1999.

Kopp, Hans. *The Last Generation Forgotten and Left to Die: Postwar Memories of a Child: The History of the Danube Swabians in Word and Pictures* . Published by Hans Kopp, 2003.

Kramar, Zoltan. *From the Danube to the Hudson: US Ministerial Dispatches on Immigration From the Habsburg Monarchy: 1850-1900. Issue 9 of State University of New York College at Buffalo's Program in East European and Slavic Studies Publications*. NY: State University Buffalo Press.

Kuper, Leo. *Genocide: Its Political Use in the 20th Century*. CT: Yale University Press, 1983.

_____. *The Prevention of Genocide*. CT: Yale University Press, 1985.

Kurapovna, Marcia. *Shadows on the Mountain: The Allies, The Resistance, and The Rivalries that Doomed WWII Yugoslavia*. NJ: Wiley, 2009.

Lituchy, Barry. *Jasenovac and the Holocaust in Yugoslavia*. NY: Jasenovac Research Institute, 2005.

Marczali, Henry. *Hungary in the Eighteenth Century*. Introductory essay by Harold W. V. Temperley. Cambridge: Cambridge University Press, 1910; reprint ed., New York: Arno Press and the New York Times, 1971.

Mentzel, Peter. *The German Minority in Inter-War Yugoslavia. Nationalities Papers* 21, no. 2 (1993): 129-43.

Mehrdad Kia. *The Ottoman Empire*. CT: Greenwood Publishing, 2008.

Merter, Ulrich. Forgotten Voices: *The Expulsion of the Germans from Eastern Europe after World War II*. NJ: Transaction Publishers, 2002.

Miller, Nicholas. *Between Nation and State: Serbian Politics in Croatia before the First World War*. Pittsburgh: University of

Pittsburgh Press, 1997.

Mocsy, A.C. *Pannonia and the Upper Moesia:A History of the Middle Danube. Provinces of the Roman Empire Series.* NY: Routledge, 1974.

Mosier, John. *Hitler vs. Stalin: The Eastern Front 1941-1945.* NY: Simon and Schuster, 2011.

Mosse, George. *The Crisis of German Ideology: Intellectual Origins of the Third Reich.* New York: The Universal Library, 1964.

Nussan Porter, Jack. *Genocide and Human Rights: A Global Anthology.* MD: Rowman and Littlefield Publishing Group, Inc., 2000.

O'Brien, H.C. *Ideas of Religious Toleration at the Time of Joseph II.* Transactions of the American Philosophical Society Retrieved 02-2012.

Paikert, Geza C. *The Danube Swabians. The Hague*: Martinus Nijhoff, 1967

Patai, Raphael. *Jews of Hungary: History, Culture, and Psychology.* IN: Wayne State Unniversity Press, 1996.

Prokle, Herbert. *Genocide of the Ethnic Germans in Yugoslavia, 1944-1948.* Donauschwabische Kulturstiftung, 2003.

Remmler, Karen. *Correspondences Between Walter Benjamin's Concept of Remembrance and Ingeborg Bachmann's Ways of Dying.* Studies in Austrian Literature, Culture and Thought. CA: Ariadne Press, 1996.

Robinson, I.S. *Eleventh Century Germany: The Swabian Chronicles.* England: Manchester University Press, 2008.

Rona-Tas, Andras. *Hungarians and Europe in the Early Middle Ages.* Central European University, 1999.

Rudiger, Hermann. *Die Donauschwaben in der Sudslawischen Batschka.* MI: University of Michigan Library, 1923.

Schindler, John R. *Yugoslavia's First Ethnic Cleansing: The Expulsion of the Danubian Germans, 1944-1946.*

Schmidt, Frank. *The Genocide of the Indigenous Ethnic Germans of Yugoslavia.* Danube Swabian periodical *Heimatbote,* Feb. 1991.

_____. *An Introduction to the Danube Swabians*.

Schmidt, Jakob. *Palanka*. Translated by Doris Feldtanzer. Unpublished manuscript.

Seton-Watson, Robert William. *Treaty Revision and the Hungarian Frontiers*. London: Eyre and Spottiswood Ltd., 1934.

Shepherd, Ben. *Terror in the Balkans: German Armies and Partisan Warfare*. MA: Harvard University Press, 2012.

Silverman, Lisa. *Becoming Austrian: Jews and Culture Between World Wars*. UK: Oxford University Press, 2012.

Singleton, Frederick Bernard. *A Short History of the Yugoslav Peoples*.MA: Cambridge University Press, 1985.

Spira, Thomas. *German-Hungarian Relations and the Swabian Problem. Eastern European Quarterly*. New York: Columbia University Press, 1977.

Springenschmid, Karl. *Our Lost Children: Janissaries?* Translated,with additional notes, by John Adam Kohler and Eve Eckert Koehler. Milwaukee: Danube Swabian Assoc. of the USA, 1981. Originally published under the title, Janitscharen? Die Kinder Tragoedie im Banat, Vienna: Eckartschriften.

Stanton, Gregory. *World Federalist Association Campaign to End Genocide*. http://payson.tulane.edu/seminars.

Starkie, Walter F. *Raggle Taggle:Adventures with a Fiddle in Hungary and Roumania*. UK: John Murray Publishers, 1933.

Stavrianus, L.S. *The Balkans Since 1453*. NY: NYU Press, 2000.

Steigerwald, Jacob. *Donauschwaebisches Gedankenskizzen aus USA—Reflections of Danube Swabians in America*. Winona, MN: Translation and Interpretation Service, 1983.

Stretenovic, Stanslav and Prauser, Steffen. *The Expulsion of the German Speaking Minority from Yugoslavia*. From the publication *The Expulsion of the German Communities from Eastern Europe at the End of the Second World War*. Published for European University Institute, Florence, Italy, 2004.

Sunic, Tomislav. *Titoism and Dissidence: Studies in the History and Dissolution of Communist Yugoslavia*. Frankfurt, New York: Peter

Lang, 1995.

Styron, William. *A Wheel of Evil Comes Full Circle: The Making of Sophie's Choice*. The Sewanee Review, Vol. 105, No. 3. Summer 1997. MD: Johns Hopkins University Press. (Eli Weisel qts.)

Swales, Martin, ed. *German Poetry: An Anthology from Klopstock to Enzensberger*. Cambridge GB: Cambridge University Press, 1987.

Szuchman, Jeffrey. *Nomads, Tribes, and the State in the Ancient Near East. Oriental Institute Seminars*. CH: University of Chicago Press, 2009.

Thompson, E.A. *The Huns*. NY: Wiley Blackwell, 1999.

_____. *Romans and Barbarians: The Decline of the Western Empire*. WI: University of Wisconsin Press, 2000.

Totten, Samuel. *Dictionary of Genocide 2 Vols*. CT: Greenwood Publishing Group, 2007.

Vardy Kumm, Otto. *Geschichte der 7. SS-Freiwilligen G.birgs-Division "Prinz Eugen."* Coburg: Nation Europa, 1995.

Vardy, Steven Bela and T. Hunt -Tooley, eds. *Ethnic Cleansing in Twentieth Century Europe*. Social Science Monographs, Boulder. Distributed by Columbia University Press, 2003.

Wachtel, Andrew Baruch. *The Balkans in World History*. UK: Oxford University Press, 2008.

Walliman, Isidor and R. Dobkowski. *Genocide and the Modern Age. Peace and Conflict Resolution Series*. NY: Syracuse University Press, 2000.

Wolff, Stefan. *German Minorities in Europe: Ethnic Identity and Cultural Belonging*. NY: Berghahn Books, 2002.

Wildmann, George, Hans Sonnleitner,Karl Weber and members of Arbeitskreis Dokumentation der Donauschwèabischen Kulturstift. *Genocide of the Ethnic Germans in Yugoslavia, 1944-1948*. USA: Danube Swabian Association of the U.S.A.

Wildmann, George et al. *Verbrechen an den Deutschen in Jugoslawien*.

PART THREE

Teaching Genocide

How do you teach events that defy knowledge, experiences that go beyond imagination? How do you tell children, big and small, that society could lose its mind and start murdering its own soul and its own future?

Elie Wiesel

Teaching Guide Copyright A. Botein, 2012

Partial List of Crimes Against Humanity

Ancient Rome:
Second Samnite War (326-304 BCE): The Romans massacred four towns and killed all of the male residents because the Samnites were considered guilty of treason.

Hannibalic Wars: The Romans enslaved 14 Italian and Sicilian towns and massacred the entire population of two other towns because the victims had changed sides or were thought to be about to do so.

Roman sacking of 72 settlements in Epirus producing 150,000 slaves.

Gallic Wars: The campaigns in Gaul led by Julius Caesar in his two terms as proconsul of Cisalpine Gaul, Transalpine Gaul, and Illyricum (58 B.C.—51 B.C.).

Armenia: The massacre of the Armenian Christians by the Turks during 1915 and 1916.

Australia: Black War between the British Colonists and Tasmanian Aborigine in the early nineteenth century.

Bosnia-Herzegovina: The genocide of hundreds of thousands of people, mainly Muslims, primarily by Serbian Orthodox Christians in Bosnia-Herzegovina during the 1990s.

Cambodia: The destruction of over one million Cambodians and others by the Khmer Rouge Communists in the mid 1970s. The Cambodian Communist Party (led by Pol Pot and other leaders) mass killing of ideologically suspect groups, ethnic minorities like the ethnic Vietnamese, Chinese (or Sino-Khmers), Chams and Thais, former civil servants, former government soldiers, Buddhist monks, secular intellectuals and professionals, and former city dwellers.

China: The Great Famine of China, which took place from 1958-61, is one of the greatest tragedies of recorded history, killing between 14 and 40 million people

Congo: The deaths of unknown millions Congolese, starting in 1885 and continuing into the twentieth century, while the *Congo Free State* (now the *Democratic Republic of the Congo*) was controlled by King Leopold II of Belgium. It was a regime of widespread forced labor, mass murder, mutilation, and torture.

Croatia: The genocide of Muslims, Roma, Serbian Orthodox, and others by Ustasia, a Roman Catholic Fascist regime that controlled Croatia from 1941-1945.

Darfur: The Sudan Liberation Army (SLA) and Justice and Equality Movement (Jem) began attacking government targets in early 2003, accusing Khartoum of oppressing black Africans in favor of Arabs. Some 2.7 million people have fled their homes since the conflict began in the arid western region, and the UN says about 300,000 have died, mostly from disease.

Dersim: Turkish massacre of Kurds in Dersim 1937-8.

Eastern Europe: The highly organized extermination of about 11 million persons by the Nazi government of Germany, including six million Jews, millions of Poles, and 400,000 Roma during WWII. There are Holocaust deniers who say it never happened.

Guatemala: Guatemalan Genocide against Maya Indians 1968-1996.
Guinea: Equatorial Guinea genocide of Bubi ethnic minority 1979.
Haiti: Dominican "Parsley Massacre" of Haitians in 1937.

Herero and Namaqua: The victims of the 1904 genocide in what is today Namibia were the Herero, who lost 80 percent of their total population. The perpetrators were the Germans. The extremism current in this episode as interpreted by a contemporary German academic may have helped fashion the race theories of Adolf Hitler. What began as a colonial war ended with what today might be termed the ethnic cleansing of the Herero. It was followed by a brutal two-year war against the Witbooi Namas in the South, which left half their population dead. As with the Herero, many were to die in labor camps.

India: Partition of India in 1947 when millions of Muslims, Hindus, and Sikhs were slaughtered.

Poland: Massacres and ethnic cleansing of Poles in Volhynia and Eastern Galicia, carried out by the Ukrainian Insurgent Army (UPA) in the Nazi occupied regions of the Eastern Galicia (1943-1944).

North Korea: North Korean Famine in mid-1990s.

Patagonia: 1870 Argentinian purging of Aborigines from Patagonia.

Philippines: Philippine-American War 1899-1902 resulted in the death of one million Philippinos.

Spain: Atrocities which occurred during and after the Fascist coup led by General Franco in 1936 with the active support of the Catholic Church and the Spanish Army, and made possible by the assistance of Hitler and Mussolini. More than 200,000 men and women were executed by the Fascist regime, and another 200,000 died in the army's concentration camps and in the villages, subjected to hunger, disease, and other circumstances. And 114,266 people simply disappeared.

Sudan: The genocide of Christians and Animists by the Muslim government of Sudan. This program continues today, though seemingly slowing down.

Tibet: Muslim warlord Ma BuFang's genocide of Tibetans.

United States: Native American Genocide: The Indian Removal Act of 1830 and the Trail of Tears; the distribution of smallpox-infected blankets by the U.S. Army to Mandans at Fort Clark was the causative factor in the pandemic of 1836-40.

Research Activities

Group Projects: Form groups of six and assign some or all of the questions and issues among the group members for oral report and/or visual presentation.

Japanese American Internment. Research the events and determine the factors which led to Japanese American internment and the impact of that experience on Japanese American families and children. Do you think that something similar to the Japanese American internment can happen again? Discuss current events: Weren't individuals from Iraq suspected of espionage and watched closely during the Persian Gulf War? Do you think those fears could have escalated and resulted in serious action? Why do you think Japanese American citizens were interned, while citizens of Italian and German descent (who also looked like the enemy) were not? Do you think Japanese Americans were fairly compensated by the U.S. government for their experience?

Armenian Genocide: What point was Adolf Hitler making when he said: "Who, after all, talks nowadays of the annihilation of the Armenians?" What were the major factors contributing to the outbreak of the Turkish genocide against the minority Armenian population? How and why was the context of World War One significant? What were the dimensions of "eliticide" and "gendercide" in the Armenian genocide? What was the role of mass deportations in the genocide? To what extent were the perpetrators of genocide brought to justice after World War One? Why weren't such efforts more successful? What has been the role of the modern Turkish state and its international supporters in denying the Armenian genocide? Are there any signs that the official Turkish position may be changing?

Cambodia and the Khmer Rouge: What was the impact of the massive U.S. bombing campaign against Cambodia in bringing the Khmer Rouge to power? What were the main features of Khmer Rouge ideology? Who were the principal targets of the regime? What is "urbicide," and what role did it play in the Cambodian genocide? What were the major mechanisms by which Cambodians were murdered between 1975 and 1979? What were the similarities and differences between Democratic Kampuchea under the Khmer Rouge, and the Soviet system under Stalin? How successful has the post-genocide quest for justice been in Cambodia?

Bosnia and Kosovo: To what extent can the Bosnian genocide be ascribed to "ancient hatreds?" What are the historical origins of the Yugoslav state? What occurred in Yugoslavia during World War Two, and how did it factor in the outbreak of mass violence in the 1990s? What role did Nationalist leaders play in the late 1980s and early 1990s? What criticisms have been made of the foreign (Western European and U.S.) role in Yugoslavia's dissolution, and during the Bosnian war of the 1990s? What was the "*gender*cidal" dimension of the Bosnian genocide? What happened at Srebrenica in July 1995, and why? In what ways was the campaign in Kosovo in 1998-99 similar to the Serbs' genocidal strategy in Bosnia? Do you think the Serbs' war against Kosovar Albanians should be considered a genocide? How successful has the post-genocide quest for justice been in the territories of the former Yugoslavia?

Holocaust in Rwanda: Who are the Hutus and who are the Tutsis? Is it accurate to talk about "ancient tribal hatreds" between these two groups? What role did Belgian colonialism play in paving the way for the Rwandan holocaust? What were the demographic, environmental, and economic factors that may have contributed to the genocide? What was the essence of the "Hutu Power" ideology advanced by extremists within the Rwandan regime? What was the impact of the invasion of Rwanda by the Rwandan Patriotic Front

(RPF)? Do you think the RPF should be credited with having stopped the genocide, or blamed for having helped to trigger it? What role did Rwandan media, especially RTLM Radio, play in the onset and implementation of the genocide? Why was the international community so unwilling to intervene to stop the genocide? What would you have done differently? Why and to what extent was an intervention eventually mounted? What similarities and differences do you perceive between the Rwandan and Jewish holocausts? In what ways might the Rwandan genocide be considered "unique?" Discuss the role of ordinary Hutus in perpetrating the Rwandan holocaust. How successful have post-genocide efforts at justice and reconciliation been in Rwanda?

Jewish Holocaust: What was the nature of European anti-Semitism, and why did it arise? What is the link between such anti-Semitism and the Nazi Holocaust against the Jews? What factors contributed to Adolf Hitler's rise to power in 1933? What was the nature of Nazi ideology, and the Nazi political system that Hitler oversaw? What was the attitude of "ordinary Germans" towards the Nazis' persecution of the Jews during the 1930s? What were the various strategies employed by the Nazis to destroy the Jews of Europe? Why was the decision made to switch from up-close executions to murder by cyanide gas? Why did the Nazis establish their network of death camps in Poland and not in Germany? What are "intentionalist" versus "functionalist" explanations of the Jewish Holocaust? How and to what extent did Jews resist the Nazis? What role did the Allies and Christian churches play during the Holocaust? Why weren't greater efforts made to save the Jews of Europe? What is the essence of "the Goldhagen debate?" Is the Jewish Holocaust "uniquely unique?"

Who were the other principal victims of the Nazis? What similarities and differences do you see between the Nazis' targeting of these victim groups and their strategies towards European Jews? What specific role did the Nazi campaign against mentally and physically handicapped people play in paving the way for the Holocaust against the Jews?

The Great Irish Famine (or Potato famine) that began in 1845, killed more than a million people and forced another million to flee the country. Seventy-five percent of the Irish who came to the U.S. ended up in New York. Using articles, books, electronic sources, examine British policies that exacerbated the situation, such as the middle man system, rack-renting practice, and a laissez-faire approach toward aiding the starving population. You might also examine the impact the immigrants had on New York and Boston and parallel the situation to twenty-first century immigration issues. Does the Irish Famine meet the definition of a genocide?

Native Americans: Notorious incidents of what we now can define as genocidal acts and crimes against Native Americans are well cited in early U.S. history, specifically, the Trail of Tears, the Sand Creek Massacre, and the massacre of the Yuki of northern California. More controversial, however, is whether the colonies, individuals, and the U.S. participated in genocidal acts as an overall policy toward Native Americans. The Native-American population decrease since the arrival of Spanish explorer Christopher Columbus alone signals the toll colonization and U.S. settlement took on the native population. Scholars estimate that approximately 10 million pre-Columbian Native Americans resided in the present-day U.S. That number has since fallen to approximately 2.4 million. While this population decrease cannot be attributed solely to the actions of the U.S. government, they certainly played a key role. In addition to population decrease, Native Americans also have experienced significant cultural and proprietary losses as a result of U.S. governmental actions. The total effect has posed a serious threat to the sustainability of the Native-American people and culture. Research the various motivations for the crimes perpetrated against the Native Americans such as colonization, westward expansion, arrogance and a sense of superiority, etc. Is it correct to refer to the plight of the Native Americans as a genocide as defined by the UN statute?

Individual Research Projects

Prepare an oral report as follows: What symptoms of intolerance towards a specific group have you observed or experienced? Describe the circumstances and how you felt.

Discuss a time you experienced prejudice or discrimination; a time you discriminated against somebody else; a time you witnessed discrimination and did nothing about it; or a time you witnessed discrimination and did something about it. What is it that leads us to act or choose not to act?

Witch Trials: Many people associate witch trials with New England Puritanism. Actually, alleged witches were burned alive over a five century interval, from the fourteenth to the eighteenth century throughout England, German, and France. Research witch trials in one of these countries.

Genocide Research: Investigate and write a paper on the history of one of the lesser-known genocides in the listing using scholarly articles, electronic sources, and/or news stories. Does it meet the definition of the word genocide and the eight stages of genocide, and/or survivor testimony?

Oral History: Interview and videotape a survivor, child of a survivor, or witness to a genocide to document that person's experience. Place it in the historical and political context of the genocide

Religious Diversity: Identify one (or two, three, etc.) major religion represented in the United States and research the history and fundamental beliefs of the religion. What myths and misperceptions do people hold about other ethnic or religious groups, and what can be done to debunk them?

Expanded Critical Thinking and Research:

A lesser-known example of a federal genocidal act against Native Americans was the involuntary sterilization of approximately 70,000 Native-American women. The federally-funded Indian Health Services carried out these sterilizations between 1930 and the mid-1970s. They were often done without informed consent, covertly, or under a fraudulent diagnosis of medical necessity. This directly contravenes the UN Genocide Convention. Destroying a group's ability to reproduce is an obvious and crude method of ensuring the inability of the group's survival. Research the history, reasons, and reactions to this violation of human rights.

Do you think that human beings are innately wired to act kindly? Or is kindness a quality that needs to be taught (nature versus nurture)?

Read the U.S. Constitution and the Declaration of Independence. Describe values inherent in these documents (e.g., freedom, liberty, justice, truth, equality). How does prejudice, discrimination, and bigotry promote values that run counter to those of these documents?

Listen to and discuss "The Sounds of Silence" (Simon & Garfunkel) and "Carefully Taught" (from South Pacific: Rogers & Hammerstein). Discuss silence, indifference, fear of new people and situations, and how we may accept others' prejudices too easily and without thinking.

What would you consider some of the strengths and weaknesses of your upbringing? If the influence of home environment exerts such a strong influence on the rest of our lives, how can a person rise above the weaknesses he or she experienced in his earlier years?

What are some ways we can teach our cultural values to our children and grandchildren so that they are interested in and prepared to pass down the same values to their children and grandchildren?

What is hate speech? Research Adolf Hitler's hate speech. What words and arguments did he use to inflame anti-Semitism? Are there any political figures today who engage in hate speech against any ethnic or religious group? What is being done, if anything, to stop it?

Internet Hate describes the rapidly expanding practice utilized by racists and extremists to place anti-Semitic, racist, and other hateful material on the World Wide Web. The growth of the Internet has enabled bigoted and sometimes violent messages to reach a much wider and broader audience than ever before. Consequently, these messages of hate have become widely accessible online—in homes, offices, schools, and libraries. Research and discuss the prevalence of and reason for hate and extremist speech on the Internet. What can be done to stop it?

Define the term "freedom of speech" as it is explained in the U.S. Constitution. Is it used to allow and excuse extremist speech? How do you relate it to hate speech that is prevalent on the Internet? Should anyone be able to say what he wants about another ethnic, national, or religious group?

How do people with dual cultural identities (Jewish-American, Irish-American, Italian-American, Hispanic-American) assimilate into American society while maintaining their heritage? Is this as important to second- and third-generation Americans as it was for the immigrant generation?

Research problems that immigrants who came to America in the late-nineteenth and early-twentieth century experienced in terms of acceptance, assimilation, and discrimination. How did they cope with the problems of living in a new land?

Does your community offer programs on stopping the hate and bullying? Speak with members of the police force and/or district attorney's office. If there is a program, gather information. If not, what kind of a program would you want to be implemented? Can the hate stop in our own backyard?

Write about a particular custom of your ethnic, religious, or national background. What is its significance? Is it important to you? Why or why not? What do you think is the importance of traditions in our life?

Research the cultural importance of music to a particular ethnic group.

What is the importance of one's cultural or national language? Should English be the only accepted language in public schools in America? Research pros and cons of this hot-button issue.

Read the story/memoir of a survivor. Put yourself in the place of the survivor. What were their lives like before the war? When the world you know is destroyed, how do you begin again? What allowed some survivors to carry on and rebuild a life after the war/genocide when others could not? How does a person transform himself—or herself—from a victim into a master of his or her own destiny? What of their old lives did they retain?

Respond to the following statement: "It's not too late to do something about the atrocities today."

Research incidents of hate crimes today; preferably those close to home. What are the similarities among the groups of individuals who commit these crimes? Who do they target? How are they similar to or different from the Nazis? What kind of actions can we take to counter these crimes? How do you answer revisionists who deny that the Holocaust ever happened?

Investigate the art and music that has been written by survivors of any genocide. Can words and images convey the evil nature of the perpetrators?

How does treating animals well foster respect for all living creatures?

Martin Buber, the Israeli philosopher, maintains that the way to approach the divine is through "becoming human." What does he mean by this, and are there other ways?

View a film based on a genocide, such as *The Killing Fields* or *Hotel Rwanda*. Write a report on how it reflects the particular crime against humanity and place it in its historical context.

What is your position on interfaith dating and marriages? What are some pros and cons?

Research and conduct interviews with your or other families

within your ancestral heritage. What contributions has that group made to America?

Genocides of Indigenous Peoples: What are "indigenous peoples?" What is the "discourse of extinction" vis-a-vis indigenous peoples? Why have so many genocides occurred against indigenous peoples worldwide? What role did genocide play in the conquest of indigenous peoples in either the Americas, Africa, or Australasia?

What is a bystander? What is an upstander? How much do you think a passive bystander is responsible for genocidal violence? Research examples of someone who put his or her life in danger and was a selfless hero during one of the atrocities listed.

According to the Genocide Convention, genocide can be against a national, ethnical, racial or religious group. The convention has been criticized for not protecting political and social groups and for not recognizing persecution on the basis of gender or sexuality. Why do you think the United Nations limited its definition of genocide? What has changed since 1948 that might merit a more inclusive definition? How might this change the obligations of member states at the United Nations?

How have attempts to address genocide in Sudan differed from past international efforts regarding genocide in other areas?

The Genocide Convention requires state parties to, "prevent and punish genocide." In the past 50 years, tribunals to punish genocide have been administering justice, and the International Criminal Court has been established. However, in the aftermath of war, the international community has recognized genocide in Cambodia, Yugoslavia, and Rwanda. Millions of people have died without intervention. In your opinion, has the Genocide Convention been successfully implemented? If not, what are some of its limitations?

All of the following important human rights treaties have committees to ensure implementation and compliance:

Convention on the Elimination of all forms of Discrimination against Women (monitored by the Committee on the Elimination of Discrimination Against Women)

International Covenant on Civil and Political Rights (monitored by the Human Rights Committee)

United Nations Convention against Torture and Other Cruel, Inhuman or Degrading Treatment or Punishment (monitored by the Committee against Torture)

What can be done to make the Genocide Convention more meaningful (especially with regard to prevention)?

In his article, "Seeking Justice in Cambodia: Realism, Idealism, and Pragmatism," Dr. Gregory H. Stanton says: "Human rights are not lost because of the absence of law, but because of the lack of political will to enforce it." Whose responsibility is it to respond to genocidal violence in another country? How do moral standards interact with legal and political standards and goals?

Do you agree or disagree with this quote, often attributed to Edmund Burke: "The only thing necessary for triumph of evil is that good men do nothing?" Explain your point of view.

He slits the wombs of pregnant women; he blinds the infants.
He cuts the throats of their strong ones...
Whoever offends the god Asshur will be turned into a ruin.
- Assyrian poem glorifying a military victory of Tiglat-Pileser I, 1100 BCE

Research a "genocide" during the Biblical/Greek and/or Roman era, and apply the following comment from The Oxford Handbook of Genocide Studies by Donald Bloxham and A. Dirk Moses. Oxford University Press, 2010: "The evidence for genocide in antiquity ranges from highly rhetorical celebrations or condemnations of the annihilation of an enemy to laconic notices about the destruction of cities, and its value is often hard to assess. Is a claim that the enemy was 'utterly destroyed' a record of genocide or a hyperbolic boast of overwhelming victory? What does it mean when cities are said to be 'razed to the ground', when so many of these places reappear in the sources only a few years later, as if nothing had happened? We do not always have enough evidence to answer such questions. Yet even when we cannot tell what reality lay behind the words, the rhetoric is valuable because it reveals ancient ideologies of genocide."

Can One Person Make a Difference? Genocide is not inevitable. Human actions lead to it, perpetrate it, and cover it up. The question, "How can genocide be prevented?" suggests that a formula, once devised, will provide the solution. But the answer, which for some is wholly unsatisfying, is that there may be no *one* answer. What is clear is that ignoring genocides by simply mentioning them in passing or weighing them in a kind of numbers game of ranking sends implicit messages that these historical events and their victims are unimportant. Why do you think it is important to "never forget?" What do you think the individual or groups can do to begin to stop the stereotyping, intolerance, and hate-based policies that create the climate for holocausts and genocide to happen? Can one person make a difference? Can you?